Do you want something to eat?" Ellie asked softly.

"Nope," Pete said.

"What then?"

He shifted on the stool so that his knees opened, and he slid her stool between them. "You."

"Me?"

"Yep," he said. His fingers played with loose strands of hair at the nape of her neck.

Ellie was so keenly aware of the pressure of his thighs on hers, she could barely speak. "With or without mayo?" she asked lightly.

He nuzzled her neck. "It's not just you, Ellie, it's this incredible smell about you—" His voice was a tantalizing whisper against the soft skin of her neck.

"Garlic?"

"—and wildflowers and blueberry jam. All sorts of wonderful, sensual things."

Ellie squirmed. "You don't make my life easy," she managed to say through lips gone dry and with a racing heart. "It was easier when I didn't like you."

He smiled, then nibbled lightly at her earlobe. "So you do like me. A start, Ellie, a definite start. . . ."

WHAT ARE *LOVESWEPT* ROMANCES?

They are stories of true romance and touching emotion. We believe those two very important ingredients are constants in our highly sensual and very believable stories in the LOVESWEPT line. Our goal is to give you, the reader, stories of consistently high quality that may sometimes make you laugh, sometimes make you cry, but are always fresh and creative and contain many delightful surprises within their pages.

Most romance fans read an enormous number of books. Those they truly love, they keep. Others may be traded with friends and soon forgotten. We hope that each LOVESWEPT romance will be a treasure—a "keeper." We will always try to publish

**LOVE STORIES YOU'LL NEVER FORGET
BY AUTHORS YOU'LL ALWAYS REMEMBER**

The Editors

FOR MEN ONLY

SALLY GOLDENBAUM

BANTAM BOOKS
NEW YORK · TORONTO · LONDON · SYDNEY · AUCKLAND

FOR MEN ONLY

A Bantam Book / June 1994

*If you would be interested in receiving protective vinyl covers for your
Loveswept books, please write to this address for information:*

Loveswept
Bantam Books
P.O. Box 985
Hicksville, NY 11802

ISBN 0-553-44219-8

Published simultaneously in the United States and Canada

PRINTED IN THE UNITED STATES OF AMERICA

OPM   0 9 8 7 6 5 4 3 2 1

ONE

Ellie Livingston grabbed a wire whisk and beat the fresh eggs fiercely. Rich, golden liquid sloshed against the sides of the cracked mixing bowl.

"Yoo-hoo, anyone home? You there, Ellie?"

"In here, Fran." Ellie wiped her hands on her smudged white apron, then grabbed a knife and began chopping a handful of pearly-white scallions into tiny bits. The knife clicked sharply against the old wooden cutting board.

Ellie's oldest sister walked into the large kitchen and eyed the dirty pots and pans piled in the sink, the half-dozen tins of spices cluttering the counter, the knives and spatulas and wooden spoons scattered across the stained Formica.

"Uh-oh," she said, backing toward the door, her eyes widening in mock fear. All the Livingston siblings knew what it meant when Ellie was in a cooking frenzy.

Ellie didn't look up. The knife clicked louder on the board.

Fran leaned against the door frame and put her hands on her ample hips. "Okay, sis, what demons are you exorcising? What did Clarence the Creep call you today?"

"After 'pretty little thing' or before 'sweet darlin'?" Ellie stopped chopping long enough to give her sister a lopsided grin.

"You pick." Fran eyed the two pies, the huge, steaming soup pot, the dozens of cookies.

Ellie paused, then forced a smile and turned toward her sister. "He, Mr. Clarence Chandler III, called me into his office at noon and told me that my application for the marketing training program had been turned down."

"Oh, hon—"

"That's what *he* said." Ellie screwed her face up into a grimace and dropped her voice in imitation of her employer. " 'Oh, honey bun, guess what?' And then he told me that he loved my sweater and that they had to cut costs, don't you see, and my goodness, what was that incredible, sexy perfume I was wearing? And they couldn't possibly afford offering an expensive training program like that to someone who was not on the ladder."

"Ladder?"

"Yes, ladder. I asked him politely, 'What ladder, Mr. Chandler?' Thinking to myself, 'Step ladder? Extension ladder? Latter Day Saints?' " Ellie began cutting again, more vigorously. "And then he said,

'Why, the *corporate* ladder, darlin'. The one that takes people up.' "

"Oh, dear. I'm sorry, El. What a crummy deal. It's so unfair."

"Yes, it is. I'm as smart as anyone in that office, Franny. I know every bit as much. But without that piece of paper that says I spent four years in some college somewhere, they don't seem to think I'm capable of adding two plus two, or, God forbid, climbing some damn ladder."

Ellie understood what her problem was. Without vanity, she knew she was both beautiful and smart, and those two attributes seemed constantly at war with each other. As her pa had always said, she had a hard time getting people to allow her brains to breathe.

Fran nodded in sympathy and said, "You need to forget about Clarence Chandler for a while. I've an idea, sis. How about if Harve and I—"

Ellie put her hands out in front of her. The knife clattered to the floor. "No! Don't even think it, Franny!"

"Now how did you know—"

"I know, I know. I know what your magic solution always is."

"Calm down, Ellie. It's been months since that *one* disaster. Are you ever going to forget it?"

"No." Ellie bent over and retrieved the knife. "I don't need your blind dates to put joy in my life, Franny. I know plenty of men."

"But the men you know have been turned down so many times that—"

"Not true. I'm busy, Franny, that's all. I'm determined that in spite of the Mr. Chandlers of this world, I'm going to get ahead. And when I want to go out, I do. But blind dates are for the birds."

"Because that one particular match wasn't made in heaven?"

Ellie laughed. "That's the understatement of the year. That particular blind date was the date from hell. The only saving grace is that I've never run into that Pete fellow again. God has spared me that, at least."

Still, she had thought about him, and that provoked her more than anything. Even all these months later she could still remember things about him, like the way he had kissed her at the end, when she'd finally made it home, soaking wet. His kiss had lingered far longer than it had any right to, first on her lips, then in her dreams.

"He was handsome," Fran said, pulling Ellie away from her thoughts.

"He was arrogant. There was something wrong, right from the start. It was as if he knew me from another life, and the other life had been awful."

"You exaggerate."

"Not so, Franny." She frowned as she tried to remember the details. For starters, he'd been a tall man, with dark hair and a dark mustache—a nice one—that he had absently stroked every now and then. But he had been kind of aloof, not speaking much. And he had looked at her with an intensity that made her uncomfortable, as if his warm brown eyes could see right into her soul.

They had met at an Italian restaurant, and everything had gone wrong, from the overzealous singing waiter whose false mustache fell into her soup, to the food being cold. More than that, the food was *horrible*. Pete—Webster, that was the last name—had recommended the place when he'd called to set up the date, said it had wonderful food. After the waiter took away her barely touched entrée, he confessed that he knew nothing about food, and his judgment might have been faulty.

To top things off, it was raining when they left the restaurant. The cab driver got lost on the way home, then crashed into the curb outside her house, which tossed her right on top of the man who had tried to keep at least two feet between them all night. And that was when he had kissed her. So odd, Ellie mused. The whole night had been so very odd.

"I do remember the date was a nightmare, at least in your opinion," Fran admitted. "So bad, in fact, that you woke Harve and me at one A.M. to tell us so. And Harvey couldn't understand it at all, because he had met the man once and he was charming. And very well respected."

Ellie shook her head. "I don't know about that, but his parting words were weird. He said something about a magazine cover. He said that the next thing he knew, he'd probably be seeing me on 'some damn magazine cover.'"

Fran wrinkled her nose. "That is strange. I'll make sure Harve checks the next guy out more carefully."

"No next guy, sweet sis. Let's talk about something important. I've a *life* to work out here. And I'll be darned if I'm going to let disastrous blind dates *or* Mr. Clarence Chandler get the best of me!"

"Atta girl!" Fran hoisted herself up on a tall stool beside the kitchen counter and reached for a still-warm cookie. "So, what are your plans? Did you, uh, how shall I say it . . . quit?"

Ellie threw her sister a dirty look, knowing the question was calculated. She had had so many jobs that her five siblings often financed nights on the town with bets placed on how long her next job would last. "No," she said, shaking her head and causing her long golden braid to sway back and forth between her shoulder blades. "Not yet anyway. But something's percolating in my head, I feel it. I'm not sure what it is yet, but soon, Fran, soon."

"Just don't be hasty, Ellie."

"I won't. But some days I'm so agitated. Remember when you were three weeks overdue with Sara? Remember how *itchy* you felt, how you paced back and forth through the infants' department at Macy's? You had this wonderful life inside of you wanting to get out. Well, sometimes that's how I feel—like it's *time*, time to get my life on a roll, time to achieve, time to give birth to something. I don't need blind dates, or irrational bosses, or dead-end jobs. I need something new, something I can sink my teeth and energy into."

Fran slid off the stool and walked over to give her sister a hug. "Well," she said, tugging on Ellie's thick braid, "if you come up short in the process, Harve and I might be able to—"

"Nope, Franny, I don't need money. Thanks to Grams leaving me this house, I have a roof over my head. And I've been able to save a little. I'm doing okay. Now pack up some of this food and get out of here, or Harve will wonder if you've run off with the mailman. And don't worry about me. I won't quit without thinking it through."

It took Ellie exactly twelve hours to think it through.

The brainstorm she was waiting for hit her at five the next morning as she pulled a perfect soufflé from the oven. She looked up and saw it clearly, the sun climbing into the warm August sky—and her future.

She'd been cooking all night, battling the demons of frustration. After two gooseberry pies, enough chocolate chip cookies to last the winter, several soups, and the best soufflé of her twenty-seven years, not only was her frustration gone, but her future was crystal clear. With an oven mitt still on one hand, she raced for the phone and dialed her boss.

When she finished speaking with him, Fran was next.

"Hello," Fran said, her voice thick with sleep.

"I have it, Fran!"

"Have what? Who? What's wrong?"

"Nothing. Everything's absolutely right! Wonderful. Perfect. I've figured out my life, and now I need the help of my wonderful family to make it all work."

"Ellie, it's the middle of the night. You're not making any sense."

"That's what Mr. Chandler said when I called him and quit."

Fran groaned.

"Could you and Harve be over here at seven tonight?" Ellie didn't wait for Fran's answer. She knew they would be there, right along with the rest of her family. Word got out quickly when Ellie had spent the night cooking.

"Okay, here's the plan," Ellie said when her family had all gathered in the narrow living room at the front of her brownstone. Fran and her husband Harve were there, along with Ellie's mother, her sisters Rosie and Emily, who were twins, and their husbands, her older brother, Sam, and twenty-two-year-old Danny, the youngest of the Livingston brood.

"Plan for what, Eleanor dear?" her mother asked.

"The plan for my cooking school," Ellie said.

Silence greeted her announcement. Ellie looked around, met everyone's eyes squarely, then smiled. "Yes, I'm going to open a cooking school. Here, take a look at this. It will explain it better." She passed around a stack of colored notebooks, and for a few minutes the only sounds in the room were the turning of pages and an occasional whistle.

Finally Fran waved her notebook in the air. "When did you do this?"

"Today. It was all in my head, and it just poured out. I used my neighbor's computer, and I might as well have been writing the recipe for fudge, it came so easily. It's all there, a sketch of the marketing plan, the improvements I'll need for my kitchen, a copy of the zoning ordinance, cost projections, mailing list ideas, everything. I will need help from all of you, though. . . ." She looked up and gave them her winningest smile. "Harvey, Eddie, and Tom"—she nodded to her sisters' husbands—"you're all so fantastic with carpentry and repairs that I thought you'd be able to whip the kitchen into shape after Sam helps me draw some plans. And Danny's already offered to help me paint this old place. And I need Ma's recipes, and tips and ideas from Franny and Rosie and Emily. It's going to work, I know it. I feel it in my bones."

There was another long silence. Then Sam, the firstborn of the Livingston clan, said slowly, "Ellie, I know you'd be a fantastic teacher. And Lord knows you have the business savvy to put it together. But there are dozens of cooking schools and classes in this town. The competition is—"

He stopped talking because the smile on Ellie's face grew broader with his every word. "Okay, El," he said, shaking his head and smiling back. "What's your trump card here?"

"Men," she said triumphantly. "*For men only!* My cooking classes will be for men who find themselves, for whatever reason, face to face with a kitchen they don't understand. Men who are single or widowed or divorced or whatever and now have to learn the ways of a blender and juicer and pastry brush. I will convince them that eating out isn't all it's cracked up to be, and that cooking can even be a form of therapy, and that there's more than one way to impress that wonderful significant other in your life, and that—" She stopped for breath, and the slight pause was all her family needed to jump in.

"Ellie, it's brilliant!" cried Rosie, but her words were nearly lost in the cacophony of sounds as everyone joined in with exclamations of approval and cries of support.

Their ideas tumbled out, one on top of another, just as Ellie had known they would. While the noise and excitement grew, she sat down in the worn wingback chair near the fireplace and listened while her family took her fledgling idea and began to nourish its growth.

TWO

"Am I ready for this?" Ellie asked herself out loud. She glanced nervously at the bright red clock on the wall. Half an hour to countdown. Then she looked around the kitchen, and her heartbeat took off. It was so beautiful. So perfect. Of course she was ready.

"You did it, sis," said Fran, coming in the back door.

"We *all* did it, Franny." It was the truth. Without the help of her family, this would still be a dream, a jumble of ideas keeping her awake at night. She spread her arms, encompassing the freshly painted kitchen in a wide sweep. "Can you believe all this, Fran?"

It had taken six back-breaking weeks and every single penny she had, but the fabulous results were laid out in front of them in shiny tiles, polished pots and pans, and freshly painted walls.

In the center of the newly designed kitchen was an island fitted with six burners and a small sink, and with a tiled counter. One wall of the kitchen had been removed. Ellie no longer had a pantry or back hall, but she did have space for four smaller work islands, each big enough for three or four people, each with space for cutting and burners for cooking. Lined up along one wall like a layout for an ad were blenders and mixers and food processors of various shapes and sizes. Some were borrowed from family members, some resuscitated from garage sale deaths. And some were brand new, the ones Ellie had taken off the hands of a couple of newly married friends, who were willing to give over their duplicate wedding presents in exchange for a meal a month for a year. The crowning touch was an enormous industrial stove that her family had pitched in and purchased for her.

Everything was in place. Now, as her mother had so aptly put it the night before, the proof would be in the pudding.

Or omelette, Ellie corrected, since that was what she was teaching in her first class. "Omelette!" she said, slapping her cheeks. "The eggs aren't here!" She rushed to the door just as her fifteen-year-old niece, Sara, walked in with two sacks full of brown eggs from the farmers' market.

Ellie relieved her of her burden and shooed her upstairs to don an apron for her role as chief assistant.

Advertising the class had been the easiest part. With a family the size of Ellie's, the contacts were endless, and a beautiful brochure, put together by her sister-in-law, had been distributed throughout all of Chicago. In spite of the eyebrow-raising price tag which Ellie had insisted would make people take her seriously, the eight-week course already had enough registrants for her to make a small profit.

"Okay, how do I look?" she asked Fran, but her mind moved immediately on to eggs and wire whisks and fresh vegetables, and she barely heard Fran's assurance that she looked, as always, absolutely beautiful. Her thick golden hair was braided to keep it back from her face, flushed today with the thrill of her venture, and her brilliant blue eyes were lit with excitement. Fran suspected that Ellie's most difficult task would be getting the men to pay attention to the eggs and vegetables instead of the teacher. But if anyone could pull this off, it was her sister Ellie.

The ringing of the front-door bell caused Ellie to jump.

Fran moved toward the back door, blowing her sister a kiss. "Break an egg, El, or whatever one says on such auspicious occasions." She disappeared out the back door, her good-luck wish hanging in the air.

Just then Sara appeared in the doorway of the kitchen with an elderly gray-haired man in tow.

He chuckled as he surveyed the room. "Well, now, I do believe I'm in the right place." His gaze settled on Ellie and he bowed slightly, doffing an imaginary hat. "Dr. Livingston, I presume."

Ellie grinned. His silvery hair looked as soft as cotton and puffed out comically behind his ears. Clear brown eyes twinkled. He introduced himself as Mortimer Van Winkle the Seventh, Tex to his friends. He was her first "For Men Only"

student, and she knew she had found her calling.

In ten minutes Ellie's kitchen was buzzing with
introductions as her students filed in one after another.
The smell of polished brass, Ivory Liquid, and fresh
paint was completely blotted out by musk aftershave,
dabs of cologne, and perspiration. The men came in
three-piece suits, jeans, and expensive khakis, and they
ranged in age from a young man of twenty-three about
to get married and determined to have a politically
correct marriage, to charming Tex, who boasted to
being *around* eighty-two or so and who was learning
to cook to please his lady love, Estelle. According
to the enrollment records Franny had put together
for her, twelve had registered for the course. Ellie
looked around and counted eleven. One no-show
wasn't bad.

With a lump in her throat as big as a batch of
bread dough, she banged two stainless steel spoons
together for attention, smiled out over the sea of
five-o'clock-shadowed faces, and began.

"Gentlemen," she said, "Welcome to 'For Men
Only.' "

She waited for the men to settle on the stools
at the work stations, then looked each one in the
eye. The trick now was to get them to listen to her
instead of looking at her. "What's a cleaver?" she
tossed out, and pointed to the young about-to-be-
married fellow.

He grinned sheepishly. "As in 'Leave It to Bea-
ver'?"

"Close," Ellie said. "I'm sure his mother used one." She held up the fat knife, and light bounced off its gleaming side. Then she rattled off the names of other essential tools, holding them, pointing to them, and quizzing the men with barely a pause between questions and answers. In five minutes foreheads were lined and eyebrows pulled together as they tried to remember the information she was showering them with.

"Good, good," she said eventually. "That's an example of how closely you'll have to pay attention to get your money's worth out of this class. Every word I say, every demonstration I give, is important. I'm going to demand a lot from you and I guarantee it will be worth the effort."

She smiled in a way that she hoped showed both charm and toughness. Gazing from one small island of men to the next, she saw that her message had gotten through. She widened her smile, lifted a huge mallet from the island, and said brightly, "Okay, gentlemen, let the games begin."

She was interrupted by the peal of the doorbell and the sound of Sara's cheerful young voice.

"Aunt Ellie," she chirped, leading a tall, dark-haired man into the kitchen. "Here's your missing student."

Ellie frowned. The man looked familiar. But who . . . ? She waited, expecting an apology for being late. No apology came.

Instead the man set his strong jaw, looked straight at her, and shrugged out of an expensive leather jacket. "Where should I sit?" he asked.

Ellie frowned again. The voice was familiar too. She motioned absently to an empty stool and pressed a hand against her rapidly beating heart. She struggled to remember the class list that Fran had printed up, but her mind drew a blank. It would come to her in time—she never forgot voices or faces—but she couldn't afford to think about it now.

"As I was saying, gentlemen," she said, pushing aside the disquieting feeling, "I'm about to show you that the kitchen is not just a place to get olives for your martinis. It's a real live stage. By the time we're through here, you'll be impressing the socks off your clients or kids or friends and lovers. Your kitchens will become your haven, your therapist."

In ten minutes she completed her walk-through of the kitchen equipment. The latecomer didn't say much, she noticed, and whenever she had a moment to sneak a look at him, he seemed to be in another world, or at least wishing he were. His eyes were half-closed, his arms folded across a broad chest. He had rolled up the sleeves of his crisp white shirt to just below his elbows, and firm muscles held the fabric tight against his skin. He lacked enthusiasm for cooking, Ellie could plainly see, but she wouldn't hold that against him. She enjoyed challenges. What bothered her, though, were the carved features, the strong chin, the long, lean body, the uncommon attractiveness. And the niggling feeling that she knew this man.

Holding an egg in one hand, a wire whisk in the other, she said, "We're going to start with omelettes tonight—nice and easy and you'll learn a lot about the equipment as we go. It's also a perfect meal because it works for breakfast, lunch, or dinner. Just jazz it up in different ways to suit the occasion.

"And they're fun to make," she rushed on, picking up steam. "You whip them up, season the eggs with some wonderful herbs, then pour the mixture into a pan and let the sizzle and smells excite your senses. Voilà, no more business headache!" She pulled a bowl from beneath the island. With smooth, easy movements of one hand, she cracked an egg into the bowl. "Once the omelette is done," she said, cracking more eggs, "just pour yourself a glass of wine, put on some music, kick off your shoes, and settle down."

They were listening intently now, Ellie could feel it. She looked up into their enraptured faces. Whoops. She was awakening the wrong senses; Franny had warned her of that.

"Okay!" she said brightly, jerking the men from their daydreams. "Enough scene setting. But trust me, guys. Cooking will be a satisfying adventure if you give it your all. It's kind of like a love affair—you jump in all the way or not at all."

The man at the back of the room opened his eyes and fixed them so intently on her, tiny goose bumps popped up all along her bare arms. Concentrate, Ellie, she scolded herself, and bit down hard on her bottom lip, carefully avoiding his gaze. "Okay, now there's a secret to cracking these eggs, folks. Tex, how about if you come up and we'll demonstrate."

Tex happily accommodated her. "I better do this right," he said, "or the yoke will be on me!"

Ellie groaned, then helped him pick out the slivers of eggshell he dropped in the bowl as he tried to duplicate her technique. She took his gnarled hand in her own, guiding him through the movements until in a short while he was cracking eggs like a pro, with only a few golden rivers running between his fingers. "Tex, you're a pro already," Ellie said.

The other men cracked their eggs into bowls with varying degrees of success, some of them laughing at their botched efforts. Ellie could feel the class pulling together as they whirled their omelette mixtures into frothy blends.

Her excitement soaring, she placed a pan on the burner, dropped in some butter, then carefully explained an easy method for clarifying butter. As she spoke, her gaze strayed once again to the taciturn latecomer, and her memory began to clear.

It was his eyes that did it. They were unusual eyes, direct and intent. Eyes that seemed to look right into her soul. Her gaze fixed on him, she lifted the heavy blue bowl, filled to the brim with uncooked eggs.

As she tilted the bowl, preparing to pour the eggs into the pan, he moved his hand, a slight gesture, an unconscious rubbing of his upper lip in the exact space where a mustache once had been.

Suddenly Ellie knew where she had seen this man before.

Her heart seemed to stop and her hands shook. "Oh, no," she moaned, before reason could handle the emotion that swept through her.

The perfectly whipped eggs, flavored with specks of fresh parsley and basil and thyme, flowed from the tilted blue bowl, out onto the stove . . . and the cooking island . . . and Ellie's brand-new tennis shoes.

She barely noticed. She was aware of only one thing: the intent, curious gaze of Pete Webster, a man she had hoped never to have the displeasure of seeing again.

THREE

After her kitchen had emptied out and Sara had done the dishes and gone home, Ellie made herself a cup of tea and calmed down.

It probably could have been worse, she mused. The spilled eggs had soaked into her brand-new Nikes, but the accident had inspired her to give the men tips on what to do when you drop your dinner just minutes before serving it to an important client or special date or prospective mother-in-law. Actually, the whole class had gone better than she had hoped—except for the disturbing gaze that had followed her around the kitchen. It was almost as if the kiss were still there, on his lips, ready to tingle and burn her.

Ellie wanted desperately for this first course to be her prototype, to go perfectly. What she didn't want was a man she had hoped never to see again reappear as one of her students. Yet there he had been, in the flesh, right in the middle of her kitchen. She snapped out the lights, checked the locks on her door, and went up the narrow stairs to her bedroom. During a hot, pelting shower, she reminded herself that it didn't matter diddly-squat—the man was there to learn how to cook, no other reason.

In spite of her clear logic, her sleep was troubled and filled with anxious dreams, dreams of fallen soufflés and burnt omelettes—and of familiar, sexy strangers slipping into the back of the kitchen with eyes as warm and rich as melted chocolate.

In the morning, while drinking strong black coffee to clear her head, Ellie called Fran. "Why didn't you tell me?" she demanded.

"Can you expand on that, El?"

"Pete Webster."

"Pete who?"

"The man in my class. The one we were discussing several weeks ago. The guy you and Harvey fixed me up with, who convinced me to swear off blind dates for the rest of my natural life."

"The charming, good-looking guy, the one who—"

"There he was, Fran," Ellie interrupted, "walking in late, sitting there in the back of the room, staring at me . . ."

Fran chuckled. "Unnerving you. Why is he taking your class?"

That's what Ellie wanted to know. She'd tried to corner him after the class, but while the others milled around, asking questions, Pete Webster had slipped out the back door and disappeared.

"I thought maybe you would know why he was there, Fran."

"I don't remember receiving his enrollment form, but his name probably wouldn't have registered anyway. He was a friend of Harvey's sister's, I think. That's how that whole blind date thing got started. Did he remember you?"

"I don't know. Probably not. It's been a long time."

"But you recognized him, even without a mustache."

"That's different. He was horrible that night and stood out. I was quiet and lovely."

"That's right, I forgot. Quiet and lovely and temperamental as hell."

"Me? Certainly not." She hadn't been very good company, that was true enough. It had been a horrible day at work. For starters, her supervisor had wanted her to meet him at the Four Seasons for cocktails—to discuss her future, he had said. Then the marketing plan she had almost single-handedly written for her boss had received accolades, and her name had never been connected to it. Certainly some of the blame for her lousy evening rested on her state of mind, but even had she been Pollyanna herself, she suspected the date still would have gone down in her memory as the date from hell.

"From what I remember Harve's sister telling me," Fran said, recalling Ellie's attention, "Pete Webster is one sexy guy who would be a major addition to any cooking course. He must have been having a bad day that night you went out. He probably had an explanation that made perfect sense, but you never gave him a chance to tell you."

"Humph."

"Well, at least you have the upper hand this time."

"You're right about that. The man's cooking skills rival Harve's."

"That bad, huh?"

"His omelette tasted like dirty tennis shoes."

Fran laughed. Ellie felt much better after she hung up the phone. She'd bet Webster had no recollection of their date, or the kiss. He probably kissed and dated dozens of women. And if he did remember, so what. What mattered was her business, her success. She wouldn't waste another minute worrying about Pete Webster.

Several miles away in a large, rambling white house, Pete Webster stood in a hot shower after a vigorous five-mile run. Running was his therapy, a necessary exertion that temporarily expunged the mayhem from his life, as he often told his twin sister, Rachel. But it hadn't worked this morning. He still felt disjointed and anxious.

It was all because of that damn cooking class his kids, with a little help from their Aunt Rachel, had given him for his birthday. He'd only gone because Rachel had convinced him he would hurt Lucy's and P.J.'s feelings if he didn't. It was all the kids' idea, Rachel had said, and they would be scarred for life if he didn't go through with it. Even worse, the kids would boycott the kitchen if he dished up one more peanut butter and egg sandwich.

So he'd gone. What a mistake. He had recognized Ellie Livingston immediately. How could anyone forget a woman like that? When she had laughed at something one of the men said, the whole evening he'd spent with her had come back in a rush of memory. That same laugh had stayed with him, haunting his dreams for weeks after their disastrous blind date. She had only laughed once that night, he remembered, at something the cab driver had said. It had been a musical laugh, the kind that got inside your head and hummed there at odd times.

Hearing her laughter again, he unfortunately remembered that entire day in excruciating detail. It was the day he had spotted his ex-wife's picture on the cover of *Cosmopolitan* at the newstand near his office. He wouldn't forget it for a long time, nor the woman, Ellie Livingston, who looked enough like his ex-wife to be her sister. They had that same untouchable, head-turning beauty, the same perfect body, the same spun-gold hair. To make matters worse, Ellie had left him burning inside, just as Elaine used to. He had been a jerk that night he took Ellie to dinner, but it had seemed beyond his control. Something about Ellie Livingston brought back things best forgotten.

Now he would be forced to sit and look at her every Wednesday night for eight long weeks—and be reminded of the woman who had nearly torn his life apart. Feeling thoroughly gloomy, he got out of the shower and dressed for work.

His daughter was already in the kitchen when he got there.

"Hi, princess." He scooped Lucy up into his arms. She was weightless, her small four-year-old body feeling lighter than the three frozen meals he had taken out to thaw for dinner that night.

"I don't want to go to preschool today," she said with ponderous sincerity.

"Why not?"

"Because I already know all that stuff." Lucy wiggled until he let her down, her reddish-gold curls bouncing in the morning sunshine. She held her head back, tilting it to one side, her pink lips forming a sweet smile. "Okay, Peter?"

"Peter?" Pete cocked one brow. "Where does this Peter stuff come from?"

"Susie calls her daddy George." A dimple flashed in Lucy's cheek.

"Hmmm. Well, I guess it's better you call me Peter than George." He pulled out a kitchen chair. "Now, how about some cereal while I check on P.J.? And then we need to start thinking about preschool. You can help the teacher with the other kids if you know it all. She'll like that." Pete checked his watch and forced himself to think ahead, to the day, the meetings that stretched out in front of him.

The slam of the front door blurred his thoughts, and a moment later his sister, Rachel, rushed into the kitchen. "Okay, how was it, and when do Paul and I get to come for dinner?" Rachel touched a finger to Lucy's nose, making her laugh.

"How did what go?" Pete asked his sister calmly.

"Don't be dumb."

Not great, he mouthed behind Lucy's head, not wanting Rachel to accuse him of destroying his tiny daughter's psyche by criticizing her birthday gift.

"I knew you'd love it," Rachel said smugly. "Taught by a woman, I hear."

Pete shook his head as the reason for Rachel's enthusiasm took familiar shape. The tie between Pete and his twin was strong. They'd spent their childhood in forged partnership against dozens of nannies and tutors while their jet-setting parents traveled the world. The bond between them had only strengthened in adulthood. When Pete's marriage fell apart, it was Rachel who picked up the pieces; and it was Rachel who now constantly and lovingly interfered in his life, wanting for Pete what she had found in her husband, Paul Winters: the perfect mate.

"You want me to marry the chef, Rachel, is that it?"

"Don't be silly, Peter," Rachel said, pushing thick reddish-gold hair behind one ear. "But I do want you to get out more. And since you refuse any efforts to fix you up—with an ardor, I might add, that is totally inappropriate—cooking classes will have to do." She picked up a dish towel and wiped milky smudges from Lucy's cheeks and chin. "So, what was it like?"

"It was—" He paused for effect, then said carefully, "not my favorite way to spend a valuable two hours."

"Nonsense. A friend of mine who's a friend of the instructor's sister said that the teacher is beautiful and smart and probably has more business sense than the bankers and lawyers and doctors who are paying outrageous amounts to take her course."

Pete frowned. "Outrageous amounts? What did this omelette-making nonsense cost?"

Rachel straightened up. "None of your business. But you mark my words, this woman is going somewhere."

Pete thought of Ellie Livingston and the way she had handled a kitchenful of male egos. He had a nodding acquaintance with several of the men he'd seen in the class, and although they were power hitters, Ellie hadn't been intimidated in the slightest. Rachel was probably right: She was as bright and ambitious as the worst of them. Ambitious women were not exactly Pete's favorite dinner course. He shrugged now, not wanting to discuss with his sister his former association with the golden-haired chef. What he wanted to do was forget about it and forget about the cooking course and forget about women who managed to exert unwanted control over certain bodily functions. Pete hated losing control, and he assiduously avoided situations that might precipitate it. So he would just hold his silence, play down the course, and by next week no one would remember that on Wednesday evenings he was supposed to be wasting his time in some woman's kitchen.

Pete had completely underestimated Rachel's staying power. At exactly seven-fifteen the next Wednesday evening she showed up at his door.

"Thought maybe you'd have problems with a sitter," she said, "it being a school night and all, so here I am, brother dear. Rachel to the rescue. Paul's out of town, I'm free as a bird, so don't hurry home." She kissed him on the cheek, flashed the dimple in her cheek, and brushed past him. "Tootles," she said over one shoulder, and disappeared into the family room to play with her niece and nephew.

Pete rubbed the back of his neck and stared after her. He was too tired to argue. It had been a hell of a day. At least the class would allow him some privacy. He'd sit in the back, block out the instruction, and maybe even get in a snooze.

When Pete walked into Ellie's kitchen a short while later, it was filled with laughter and talk and the banging of pots and pans. In the background was music. So much for the snooze. He edged his way around a squat man whom he recognized from a business journal as having made a fortune in bathroom fixtures. "For Men Only" was getting its share of noted Chicago bachelors.

"Armco," he heard the beautiful Ellie Livingston say as he took his seat at the back work station. "It's a steal at fifteen and had an incredible year last year. Next year will be even better. It's small but powerful and has great growth potential."

Stocks? This woman was giving Harold Evans, an accountant with one of the largest accounting firms in Chicago, advice on stocks? He started to smile at her folly, but it was immediately wiped away when he realized Harold Evans was listening, even jotting down a couple of things she was saying. Pete frowned at his own irritation. Why was it he wanted Ellie Livingston to do something inane, to say something horrible that would immediately and justifiably wipe her—and the taste of her lips—completely and totally out of his mind?

"A problem, Pete?" Ellie asked, apparently noticing the expression on his face.

He looked across the sea of men and zeroed in on the forced smile she threw his way. "No problem, Miss Livingston."

"You may call me Ellie," she said cheerfully. "The kitchen is no place for formality." She motioned toward some handouts at his work station. "And you might read over those sheets on safety in the kitchen. Most of the others arrived a little early and got a head start on you."

He nodded, picked up the paper, and began to read. Did she remember him? A woman like her probably had six dates a weekend. Great for her. Great for him. He didn't want her remembering him.

"Pete?"

He glanced up to see Ellie standing a few feet away. All the other men were looking at him.

"We were discussing," Ellie said, "why people are taking this course. What brought you our way?"

The chuckles around him grated like sandpaper on glass. And her smile. Oh, it was beautiful, all right, but he didn't need this. Not the laughs, not the attention, and certainly not the tightening in his groin.

Ellie stepped closer, and he could smell her fragrance, the clean scent of wildflowers. The tightening in his groin intensified. "I'll be damned if I know why I'm here, Ms. Livingston," he said, his smile tense. "I thought maybe you knew."

She laughed, that wonderful laugh that made him think of wind chimes singing in a summer breeze.

"No, I don't know what's in your head, Pete," she said.

Thank God, he thought. At that moment his head was filled with an array of conflicting images. Half had him sweeping her away to explore the second floor of the brownstone, and the other half suggested he slip out the door and run like hell. None had much to do with cooking, at least not the conventional kind. He forced away the images and focused on the topic at hand. "Actually, I'm here because my kids think I'm a rotten cook. This course was a birthday present from them."

Kids. Ellie nodded, then moved on to the man sharing Pete's island. Her mind stayed on Pete, though, turning over the new information. Thinking of him as a father lent a vulnerability to him that disconcerted her. She was already having trouble with his eyes and his lips; now she'd have fatherhood to contend with as well.

"Okay, men," she announced when she returned to her island. "Tonight's class is designed to cure board-room blues. Tonight you"—she looked at each man, skipping over Pete as if he had a disease—"are going to become experts on marinating chicken breasts."

"Marinating breasts . . . interesting idea," murmured Oliver Carter, a tall, thin banker with manicured fingernails.

Ellie wasn't surprised at the comment. She knew Oliver's eyes had spent a lot more time on her derriere than on kitchen tools in the first class. But he wasn't a bad sort, she had determined; he was simply uninformed. She could handle him easily, because in this kitchen she was manager, supervisor, president, and department head all rolled up into one. In this kitchen she set the rules. She flashed Oliver a smile and insisted he come up for the first demonstration, making sure he had the clumsy job of cutting the meat in half and pulling out all the bones.

The others laughed at the mess he made, but it was all good-natured, as Ellie had known it would be, and just the right way to rid the recipe of sexual innuendos. Even Oliver laughed.

The two hours flew by, and with the exception of Tex's breast flying across the room when he attempted to flip it over in the champagne marinade, and Pete's meat burning to a disgusting black lump because he forgot to remove it from the broiler, there were no major disasters. The smoke alarm went off only once, and no one tried to leave early. At the end of the two hours, after they had dined on chicken breast in champagne sauce, Ellie gave the class a B-plus, wished them a good week, and ushered them out the door.

She sent Sara home, too, to study for a chemistry test, and faced the kitchen, cluttered with pots and pans and sticky cooking utensils, alone. Messy, she

thought, but she was wound up, and cleaning the
kitchen would help calm her.

She was actually making a go of her own cooking
school! Fran was already getting inquiries about the
next course. If this first one continued to go well, she'd
probably have more business than she could handle.
The only stumbling block in the whole scenario was
Pete Webster, and that was one of her own making.
Strictly hormonal, she told herself. Easily handled.

She walked across the kitchen, picking up empty
wineglasses as she went. At Pete's work table she
paused. There in the center, next to his plate of
charred chicken breast, was a black wallet. She picked
it up, lifted it automatically to her nose to smell the fine
leather, then flipped it open. Peter Langston Webster,
the driver's license told her.

She knew his name, so why did picking up his wallet cause such odd sensations inside her? Ellie frowned, snapped the wallet shut, and left it on her table.

She remembered seeing Pete pull out his wallet to
give a business card to another man in the class. Obviously he had forgotten to put it back in his pocket.
She'd call later and tell him it was here.

She slipped off her apron, poured herself a glass
of wine, and took a deep breath. "Five minutes for
me," she announced to the empty room, and sat on a
stool, her wineglass in front of her. She thought back
over the evening, the food, the men . . . and the wallet.
Such a nice-looking wallet.

Two fingers walked over and lightly touched its
sleek black surface. It was smooth as glass, beautiful,

rich leather. Expensive. But she would have expected that. Something about Pete Webster said as much. So he was probably successful, probably had a III after his name. What did any of that matter? Pete had still been a dud of a blind date. Forgettable. Well, obviously not exactly forgettable, but that was because of his rudeness.

She stared at the wallet again, awash in frustration and curiosity. What was it about this man? she wondered, rubbing the smooth leather with her fingertips. Quickly, before her conscience could step in, she opened the wallet again. After all, drivers' licenses weren't exactly private pieces of information. Didn't she flash hers in front of every Tom, Dick, and Harry when she wrote a check?

The license told her Pete was thirty-six, that his physical facts matched what she had already observed, and that he lived in an upper-class suburb of Chicago. The mug shot picture didn't do him justice, although it confirmed he was the mustached Pete Webster she'd met months ago.

"Well, what do you think?" The deep, lazy voice floated toward her from the door of the kitchen.

Ellie jerked her head up and dropped the wallet as if it were on fire. She stared at the figure leaning against the door frame. "How long have you been there?" she demanded. "Don't you knock before barging into people's homes?" She drew her eyebrows together and rose from the stool.

Pete didn't move. His arms were folded across his chest and his head was leaning against the door frame. He looked far too comfortable, she thought. And there was a small smile playing around his lips.

"I suppose you came for this," she said, flapping the wallet in the air, then sitting down again.

Pete didn't bother to answer. The kitchen was shadowy, with only a few lights on, but Ellie was lit by a single spot over the island. Damn, she was beautiful. The light fell across her thick hair, highlighting streaks of bronze and gold. A loose lock waved across her flushed cheek. She had removed her apron, revealing a plain white oversized cotton blouse, the sleeves rolled up and several buttons undone at the neckline, and jeans. It might as well have been an outfit out of Victoria's Secret, considering the effect it had on him. He wondered if she was aware of her sensuality. It oozed like honey, sweet and thick, naturally, without intent. He took a deep breath to try to dampen his rising libido, and promptly coughed.

"Would you like a glass of water?" she asked.

He nodded, strode across the kitchen, and poured himself a glass from the water cooler. Cold water would help, but more in the form of a shower. "We've met before, you know," he said tersely.

She sat still, not responding.

He remained in the shadows by the water cooler, looking at her. He wanted to leave. Damn, she radiated danger. But he couldn't take his eyes off her. "You're not the kind of woman easily forgotten," he said finally.

"Probably because you were so crazy about me," she said.

He half-smiled.

She smiled in return, cautiously.

When Ellie smiled, the images of his ex-wife disappeared, and that was a relief. Ellie was every bit as beautiful—model perfect, as Elaine's admirers had repeated ad nauseam—but there was a light in Ellie's smile, a brilliance that made him want to shut his eyes against its effect at the same time as it drew him in. Hell, maybe she was a witch.

"That night is kind of a blur to me," he said, only half-lying. He *was* blurry on what they ate, what the weather was, what the waiter looked like. "But I do remember that you didn't seem to be having the time of your life."

"The evening was a mess, and it followed an equally bad day."

What an understatement, Pete thought. His day hadn't been bad; it had been a disaster. When he had seen Elaine's breasts heaving off the cover of the magazine that morning, he had stormed into his office, insulted a client, and irritated everyone around him until one of his partners had the good sense to set him straight. The one thing he hadn't needed to end the day was a date with another beautiful woman. The similarities between the two women, though, were fading quickly.

"The Fates," Ellie said. "They must have been conspiring against us. Sometimes they know best."

"I suppose." He took a long swallow of the cold water, concentrating on it as it slid down his throat, willing it into other parts of him. Maybe he'd been away from women too long. Something in his system was going haywire. He didn't know this woman, didn't want to know her, and she was turning him on like fireworks on the Fourth of July.

She must have sensed his attraction to her, for she abruptly, sharply asked, "Did you think you could disguise yourself by shaving off that mustache?"

He lifted one brow. "No," he said calmly. "I shaved it off to be sure it never fell in anyone's soup."

She turned away, but not before he glimpsed her smile. She walked over to the sink and grabbed a towel. "Here," she said, tossing it to him. "I've got work to do here. A business to run. If you're going to take up space in my kitchen, you might as well get working."

Before Pete knew what she meant, Ellie had turned on every light in the kitchen, filled the sink with hot sudsy water, and donned long green rubber gloves. He had the feeling that any move short of drying dishes would invite disaster. He could almost feel the slippery gloves around his neck. She had spunk, that much he'd say for her.

"A bad day explains our disastrous date," she said, her head bent slightly as she concentrated on a large skillet, "but what's the explanation for you not wanting to be in my course?"

"Is it that obvious?" he asked, taking the dripping skillet from her gloved hands.

"Obvious? The scarlet letter was never so obvious."

"Cooking isn't exactly my forte."

"That's an understatement. You're a terrible cook, Mr. Webster."

"What happened to the kitchen being no place for formality?"

"Right. Pete, then." With the back of her gloved hand, she brushed a tendril of hair from her face.

Pete watched, fascinated. A puff of soapsuds rode the crest of her cheekbone now and shimmered in the light. It dissolved slowly, leaving behind a sheen on her cheek.

"I need another glass of water," he said gruffly. He set down the frying pan and strode across the room.

Ellie glanced over at him when he returned to the sink. He was certainly a moody sort of man, she thought. "I think I'll use you as my prototype student," she said.

"You think you can teach me?"

"I can teach anyone to cook. I'm excellent at what I do."

"Have you been doing this for a long time?"

"No. This is my first class. I opened this school," she continued, "because I wanted my own business. I found the business world a terribly unfair environment for a woman. Not for all women maybe, but for me at least. So I left it and am using my business expertise to build my cooking courses."

"And you think there's enough of a market?"

"Yes. Here, this is the last one." She thrust a heavy cast-iron pot into his hands and drained the water from the sink. While he finished drying, she bustled around the kitchen, straightening utensils, checking supplies, folding aprons.

He watched her, fascinated, wanting to touch her. She moved with great efficiency, no wasted, fluttery motions, always graceful. He could watch her for hours, he mused, her incredible body, her gorgeous face. He was even intrigued by her one sign of nerves, the way she nibbled on her full lower lip.

"Will this remain a one-woman operation, or will you hire other teachers?" he asked, reluctant to end the evening.

"Down the road I'll hire others, but I need to perfect the prototype first."

"You sound determined."

"I am," she said, turning toward him. Her eyes were large, round, showing surprise at his comment. "Failure is not on the agenda." She smiled, and walked briskly across the room. "It's time for you to leave now, Pete. Thanks for your help with the dishes."

She stood at the back door, all business. One hand rested on the handle of an umbrella that protruded from the top of the cylindrical brass stand.

Pete dropped the towel on the table and slipped his wallet into his back pocket. He was puzzled by his strange reaction to this woman who had so disturbed him those months before. She still disturbed him, but in a different way now—a way that had more to do with her and less to do with Elaine.

It meant nothing, he told himself. And the fact that he wanted to rub his hands along the smooth skin of her arms and trace a line across her lips and up over the gentle curve of her cheekbone . . . that meant nothing, too, only that he was tired and hadn't been with a woman in a long time.

Then he spotted the white knuckles of her hand where she grasped the umbrella handle, and he knew with utter certainty that if he were to touch Ellie, even in the slightest gesture of wonderment, he would definitely be touched in return, and not in a pleasant way.

He strode across the room, smiled at her, then let his gaze drift down to her hand. He nodded, as if they shared an intimate understanding. "A woman can't be too careful," he murmured, and walked out into the warm, dark night.

Rachel met him at the door. "Peter, what in heaven's name kept you?" Her reddish brows were lifted clear up into thick, wavy bangs that fell carelessly across her forehead.

Pete stood just inside the door, his hands shoved into the pockets of his pants. He frowned in intense concentration, as if Rachel had just asked him to explain one of Einstein's theories.

"It's not a difficult question, Peter," she said with some amusement. "What's wrong with you, anyway?"

He shrugged and allowed the smile to come back, the one that he had carried away from the tall brownstone on Elm Street.

"I'm not a very good cook, Rachel," was all he could manage as an explanation. "But I'll certainly get better. You can count on that."

FOUR

"No," Ellie said. "It's out of the question. I can't go out to dinner with you." She bent her knees and slid down the wall until she was sitting on the floor in her kitchen, the phone cord stretched to its limit.

"What?" Pete was damned if he knew why he had called her, but a week of thinking about her, a week of feeling distracted at meetings and out of sorts late at night when he slumped, alone, in front of the television, had made him believe it was a good idea. His inability to concentrate on the cooking lesson the night before—an inability caused by his fascination with the teacher—had convinced him. Maybe going out together would remind him of all the reasons their blind date had been such a flop. Then he could get her off his mind and move on. It was a logical thing to do, but he hadn't considered being turned down. Pete Webster had never been turned down for a date in his life. "Why?" he asked, the surprise audible in his voice.

"Because you and I don't have much in common," Ellie said. She stared at a tiny crack in the far wall and nibbled on her lower lip.

"That's probably true. But I'm not asking for a commitment here, just a companion for dinner."

"I don't think we even like each other."

"How will we know that unless we spend some time together?"

"We tried it once."

"A lifetime ago."

"I don't think it's a good idea—" But she couldn't go any further, because she didn't know why it wasn't a good idea. It was simply instinct, the echo of a small voice deep down inside of her that said, "Ellie, don't do this. It will change things, cause problems. . . ."

"You're right," Pete said affably. "It's probably not a good idea. But we'll go anyway, then we'll know for sure, and we won't have to think about it anymore."

"I haven't been thinking about it."

He went on as if she hadn't spoken. "Besides, I don't like owing people, and I owe you a meal."

"You don't owe me anything, Webster."

"I feel a little intimidated," he said, changing the subject slightly, "taking a gourmet out to eat."

"Don't. I rarely eat out, so going anywhere is a treat."

"I suppose you'll insist the place has a mustached fiddler—"

Ellie laughed. She brushed a few stray hairs back from her face, folded her legs under her, and shook her head. The guy was persistent, that much she'd give him. "Okay, Webster, what the heck. I have to eat. It might as well be with you."

"Careful there, Ms. Livingston. Don't let your enthusiasm run away with you."

His teasing was surprisingly gentle, and Ellie smiled, even when the voice inside her, the one she was struggling to avoid, grew louder.

"How about Saturday, around eight?" Pete said.

"Fine. How about we make it breakfast? And eight would be fine." The words came out, not planned. Instinct again, she decided. Or maybe her guardian angel. Her horoscope had warned her to be wary of moonlight encounters this month. Breakfast would be perfect.

"Breakfast?" Pete said.

"The most important meal of the day. Do you already have plans?"

Pete frowned. Hadn't he called her? Somewhere along the way he had lost the upper hand. He'd have to get it back. "I'm not my most charming at that hour," he said.

"But certainly equal to what you are in the evening," Ellie said brightly, and hung up.

Ellie woke up at five on Saturday morning and got her three-mile run in before the sun blistered the pavement. The sudden September heat wave had wilted the city along with her already drooping enthusiasm to see Pete Webster. Wasn't she mixing business with pleasure? She had asked Fran the night before. Fran had been no help. She had called Ellie a hermit, a recluse, and told her all work and no play was the kiss of death. To what? Ellie had asked, but Fran had only sighed in exaggerated exasperation.

As Ellie showered away the residue of her run, she decided she was worrying too much. What damage could a couple of hours with Pete Webster cause? None whatsoever, she answered herself as she slipped into shorts and a scoop-neck T-shirt. She had barely run a comb through her damp hair when she heard a car pull up. With an expertise born of always being short of time, she wound thick handfuls of hair into a braid, grabbed a faded string bag, and flew down the stairs.

Pete was standing on the top step outside her front door, his hands in the pockets of his khaki slacks, sunglasses balanced on top of his thick, wavy brown hair. "Hi," he said.

For a moment Ellie was speechless. She should have been prepared by now for the effect he always had on her—the way he scrambled her thoughts, made her feel weak and slightly disoriented. Maybe she should donate her body to the Kinsey Institute, she thought, for sex research. Something was peculiar when a man she had written off as the king of bad dates could make her feel this way.

"Are you all right?" Pete asked her. His gaze moved involuntarily, down long, tan, gorgeous legs, then back up to her face, free of makeup, her cheeks flushed by nature. That was another difference from Elaine, he thought, the lack of makeup.

Ellie used hardly any, and the effect was refreshing and beautiful.

"I'm fine," she said. "Hungry, that's all."

"Good, let's go, then. Any preferences?"

"Yes," Ellie said, and followed him out to his top-of-the-line Ford Explorer. Harvey would give his eyeteeth for one, she thought as she sank into the buttery-soft leather seat. "I would have imagined you to be driving a Porsche or Jag."

"See how you misjudge me?" Pete decided not to mention the racing-green Jag in his garage. He put the Explorer in first and pulled away from the curb.

"Turn left at the fire station," Ellie directed, then settled back, resting her head against the seat. "I suppose you're right about my being judgmental. I've judged you on one forgettable night and your horrible cooking. Maybe that's not fair."

Pete just smiled. Her perfume—or was it shampoo?—wafted through the vehicle. It was clean and crisp, a natural smell, not cloying or pretentious. Nice, he thought.

"Turn right at the next corner," Ellie said.

"Where are we going?" he asked as he rounded the corner. "The Four Seasons has a good brunch—"

"The Four Seasons Hotel?" She looked incredulous. "In my shorts and faded tee? No." She laughed. "I need to buy some things at the farmers' market. I thought we could just grab something there." She leaned forward and pointed out another turn.

"I thought I invited you out to breakfast. What is this?"

"You picked last time, remember? Besides, the market has great food. Trust me."

"Not a simple request," he murmured as he parked.

They walked out into the crowded street where vendors were selling their goods to a swelling crowd of serious food shoppers. Sweet and pungent smells—fruit and earth and vegetables—mingled together in the warm air, and Ellie paused to breathe it all in.

A step behind her, Pete frowned. He had left the kids with a sitter to go grocery shopping in the heat? But then he looked over at Ellie and his irritation faded. She was like a kid in a candy store, her eyes bright, her step lively, and her face lit with anticipation.

"I love it here," she said, her gaze darting from one display to the next.

Pete watched as she picked up a head of lettuce, her fingers doing an examination that would do credit to a surgeon. Finally she nodded approvingly, paid the vendor, and dropped the lettuce in her string bag. At the next stand the farmer recognized Ellie and tipped his faded hat in a friendly greeting before claiming in poetic terms that his zucchini had been grown just for her.

At the end of the first row of stands, Ellie lifted a handful of fresh cut flowers from a fat silver tub. "Beautiful," she murmured, burying her nose in the fragrant bouquet.

Pete was bewildered by Ellie Livingston. Just when he thought he had her figured out, she did something unexpected like smelling flowers or teasing a farmer, and he turned to mush. "When do we eat?" he asked finally as her bag began to bulge with fresh produce.

"Right now." She hooked her free arm through his and led him across the road to a small café with a blue awning and several small tables out in front. "The waffles here are to die for."

The waitress was an elderly woman who greeted Ellie with open arms. "Your usual, my deary?" she asked.

"Of course, Edith. And the same for my friend here."

The woman nodded and swished back into the tiny café. Pete frowned at Ellie. "How do you know what I want for breakfast?"

"Do you know that you frown too much? Some day those furrows will stay there permanently, and then what?" She pulled a daisy out of the bouquet in her sack and handed it to him. "Here, smell this. It will make you feel better."

"I feel fine."

"But you don't like a woman ordering for you, is that it? Well, you ordered for me last time. It's my turn."

Before Pete could respond, the smell of sweet maple syrup distracted him.

A second later Edith's plump hands were setting a thick blue-edged plate in front of him. Pats of butter melted slowly into the crisp tan squares of the largest waffle he had ever seen. It filled the entire plate from rim to rim. A bowl of chilled strawberries, tall glasses of freshly squeezed orange juice, and a platter of thick, moist slices of honey-baked ham completed the feast. He grinned in spite of himself.

"I told you so," Ellie said smugly, and closed her eyes while she savored the sweet syrup that saturated her first bite of waffle.

For the next ten minutes Pete ate in silence. The tastes overwhelmed him with memories of a summer week he and Rachel spent with one of their nannies at her family home in Wisconsin. The cooking had been like this—homemade, simple, and memorable. It had been the best food he had ever tasted. When they had returned to the big house in Winnetka—the expensive suburb where they lived—and described it to the French chef their parents employed, he had tried gamely to duplicate it. He only came up with thin little pancakes smothered in a horrible orange syrup. Pete's thoughts turned to his own kids, who'd had their share of frozen waffles, but never anything like this.

"A penny for your thoughts," Ellie said.

"Edith's waffles are fantastic. I'm going to bring my kids down here some Saturday."

"Kids love the market, at least my nieces and nephews do."

"Do you have any children of your own?" he asked.

"I thought I'd be old-fashioned, do it in the normal sequence."

"I thought maybe you'd been married."

"No, not me."

Pete watched as her tongue captured a glistening drop of syrup from the corner of her mouth. Shifting in his chair, he forced himself to concentrate on talk. "I'm surprised that you're not married."

"Why in heaven's name would that surprise you?"

"Because you're beautiful." He immediately wished he could take the words back, but they were already out there, hanging between them. "I mean—"

"Don't apologize, Webster." She stabbed a piece of waffle and chewed it vigorously, then looked at him. "But don't say foolish things like that again. Marriage and looks have absolutely nothing to do with each other. For years, men I've met and worked with have equated the two—if you're pretty, then get married. Make some man happy. Leave success to the less endowed. So dumb. Such garbage!"

Heads turned as her voice lifted. She blushed slightly and continued in a softer voice. "What I mean is—"

"I get the picture," Pete said. "But be honest, Ellie. You are beautiful. And people—women *and* men— notice beauty."

She frowned. He wondered if she was trying to disguise her looks in order to overcome this formidable handicap she had—one many women would have given fortunes for. But then her brow smoothed, her eyes lit up again, and she smiled. "Don't mind me. I get a little crazy about some things."

He could relate, Pete thought. The heat of the sun was doing crazy things to him now. And to Ellie. Her T-shirt was damp, clingy, and a scattering of freckles had appeared on her upper arms and across her chest. He wanted to touch them. Instead he ordered coffee, tall mugs with a hint of fragrant chicory, and sat back in the chair. The sun beat down on them. From behind them came the pleasant noise of bustling crowds and loud vendors selling their harvest. And here he sat in the scorching heat, with this gorgeous creature . . . and the best waffles he had ever tasted.

Sometimes life surprised him.

"Tell me about your kids," Ellie said.

She looked him directly in the eyes when she spoke. For most women, asking about his kids was a perfunctory question. With Ellie, though, it seemed vitally important.

"My kids," he said, wiping the dampness from his neck with his napkin. He smiled. "Well, my kids are great. Lucy is four going on twenty-four, and P.J. is seven."

"Do you see them often?"

Pete paused, then realized what she was asking. "I live with them. They live with me. Their mother is gone."

"Oh." *Gone where?* rattled around in Ellie's head but never made it out. The look on Pete's face stopped the words, a stern, end-of-subject kind of look. "Well," she said instead, "I guess I've done some stereotyping myself. I didn't figure you for the single-father type at all."

"And how did you figure me?"

She half-closed her eyes. "I figured you for a moody playboy at first. Then, when you showed up in the cooking class, I figured you for a moody playboy who didn't know how to cook."

"And now?"

"Now I figure you know how to cook—a little— and you're probably not a playboy in the usual sense of the word."

"Which is . . ."

"A man about town, bachelor of the month."

He nodded. "Interesting. But I'm still a playboy? Still moody?"

"An eligible bachelor, probably, but the playboy part is up for grabs. Children can put a damper on certain lifestyles. Moody?" She shrugged. "Yes."

His laugh was low. "Okay. Enough about me. Tell me what Ellie Livingston is all about."

Ellie swallowed her last bite of waffle. "Me? No secrets here, Pete. I run a cooking school, and my profession is very important to me. I work hard, I'm good at what I do, and I expect to build this enter- prise into something bigger. I have clear-cut goals for myself, short-term and long-term."

Pete moved the knife around his plate. "You're career-minded, I take it."

"You say that as if it were a disease." She frowned. Where had that happy, utterly satiated feeling gone?

"Sorry. I didn't mean it that way."

"What do you do professionally, Pete?"

"I'm a partner in an ad agency."

"Partner . . . so you work hard."

"Of course."

"And your company is important to you?"

"Sure, but—"

"Well, so is mine, Pete. And that's all there is to it."

She kept her voice level, but Pete sensed the controlled temper behind her words. Damn, even that was arousing. She was a temptress—a career-minded temptress. "You're a feisty little thing, aren't you?"

"I'm not a little thing."

"I think somewhere between the waffles and the great coffee, this conversation took a bad turn, and I'm not exactly sure why."

"I think I know. I think there are some basic things about you that I don't like, and the feeling is mutual. That makes it easy for us to push each other's buttons." She rested her elbows on the table, her chin on her hands.

"Interesting theory." Pete tried to focus on something other than pushing Ellie's buttons.

"You remind me sometimes," she went on, "of things I disliked intensely in the corporate world."

"That's not good."

"No."

He allowed his gaze to travel over her. Her hair was slightly damp from the heat, her cheeks rosy. "Do I remind you of anything you do like?"

"What a question, Webster."

"And the answer?"

She laughed. "Sure, there are things about you I like. My mother always taught us that *everyone* has some good in them. With some people, you have to look harder for it than others."

"I'm touched. And what do you like about me?"

She paused, scrutinized him, then said carefully, "I like your eyes. You have great eyes, Pete."

"I suppose that's enough to carry this relationship for a while."

"Five minutes maybe."

"I'll have to come up with some other fine qualities pretty quick."

"I'd say so, yes."

They were both smiling, enjoying the nonsense that had replaced the tension of a moment before. And they both acknowledged silently that they were, against their better judgment, enjoying each other.

Ellie thought back often to her morning with Pete during the rest of the weekend.

That Saturday night, she went out with a man she dated occasionally, a date she had agreed to weeks before. Although he was perfectly pleasant, and the Second City performance was entertaining, her thoughts kept returning to Pete—to his warm brown eyes, to his irritating comments, to his body, his voice, and to the nice way he laughed when she said something funny.

She tried to tell herself that she was simply fascinated with the contradictions, that figuring out Pete was like reading a mystery. Once she knew him better, the intrigue would disappear. Still, she wasn't able to keep him far from her thoughts the whole night long, and when her date dropped her off early, planted a chaste kiss on her lips, and disappeared, she felt guilty. She had certainly shortchanged the man, and she didn't like to do that with people.

But the guilt was forgotten when she walked into the house and saw the red light flickering on her answering machine. She slipped out of her shoes and punched the Play button.

There was no identifying name, just the now-familiar deep, rolling voice saying without preamble, "Okay, how about this for good qualities? I coach a kids' basketball team once a week and never forget my sister's birthday. Add those to the list and see what we come up with. I'll check later. Good night."

Ellie took the message to bed with her. Later she blamed his words for the all-night adventures that filled her dreams, although they had very little to do with birthdays or little kids' basketball games.

FIVE

The Saturday morning breakfast was followed two days later by lunch at a café in Old Town. Pete explained to her that he was working his way through the hours of the day. Perhaps high tea would be next. And Ellie, in spite of herself and the fact that she didn't like tea, thought it just might be a good idea.

Thoughts of high tea, however, were put on the back burner the next day when Ellie received a call from a reporter with a local newspaper.

The woman said her name was Cukie LaCrosse, and she wrote for the Sunday magazine section of the paper. She wanted to interview Ellie and write an article on "For Men Only." Visiting a class, Cukie said, was the best way to do it, because she wanted some pictures to go along with the article.

"I suppose we could arrange something," Ellie said, trying to keep the excitement out of her voice. They made arrangements for Cukie to come to the Wednesday night class next week, after Ellie had had a chance to discuss it with her students. If Cukie wanted pictures, the men would have to agree.

The class was enthusiastic. After several weeks under Ellie's tutelage, the men were not only beginning to cook edible food, they had received stock tips and marketing advice and were absolutely convinced that Ellie's beauty was simply the tip of the iceberg. If an article and pictures would help advertise her courses, they'd pose nude, Tex said, patting his ample belly.

Ellie hugged him, then wondered out loud where Cukie LaCrosse had heard about the course.

Tex beamed. "Estelle," he said proudly.

"So that's it!" Ellie grinned. "This kind of publicity is something I can't afford to buy, Tex. Please thank Estelle."

"Well, she raves all up and down the lakeshore about you, sugar!" Tex boomed.

"Tex, I don't *know* Estelle," Ellie reminded him. "How can she rave about me?"

"Estelle knows you, buttercup. She knows you through the meals I've been fixing for her. I sent her cook on a month's vacation, and I'm having the time of my life. Estelle thinks I'm Pierre Franey, Julia Child, Craig Claiborne, and Wolfgang Puck all rolled up into one fantastic bundle. And you know what that means. . . ." His eyes rolled heavenward, and Ellie laughed.

"Anyway," Tex continued, "Estelle knows this writer gal and says she's always looking for something new on the society circuit."

"If there's anything I'm *not*," Ellie said, "it's society news, Tex."

"Maybe not, peaches, but you have some of the most well-known names in Chicago signing up for your classes. And people think that's mighty interesting."

"Well, whatever the reason, I'll take the publicity. The price is right."

The door slammed, and Pete strode into the room.

"Sorry I'm late," he said.

Ellie had noticed his empty place earlier and allowed herself one anxious moment about it. Then she had forced the thought away. It didn't matter, she'd told herself. Seeing him, though, made her realize that it did matter. *He* mattered, somehow, even though she didn't want him to. Hearing his voice unexpectedly caused her stomach to flip, and all the rationalizing in the world couldn't do a thing about it.

His eyes met hers and held them for a moment in silent greeting. Then he turned to greet the others.

"Our Ellie's going to be famous," Tex told him, then filled him in on the reporter's visit.

Pete smiled at Ellie, but his expression, she thought, was subdued. Maybe he didn't like having his picture taken. Well, that was okay. She'd be aware of that and steer Cukie to someone else if she targeted Pete. "Don't worry, Pete," she said out loud. "We'll protect you from the glare of publicity."

Pete allowed her misinterpretation of his feelings to go by. For reasons he didn't quite understand, Ellie's success had an odd effect on him. It was such an irrational thing, he refused to pay it any attention.

He tuned back in to Ellie as she asked for their help. "It's going to be up to you men to see that the article is a good one. You're the proof of my pudding. So no messing up or burning meat next week."

"We need to behave? You didn't tell me that," Tex said, a twinkle in his eye.

"Darn right," Ellie said. "I'll pick something you can't possibly mess up—"

"Jell-O?" Pete suggested.

Ellie laughed, then waved them to their places. "Enough about next week. We have work to do *now*. I'm going to challenge the heck out of you tonight."

She had purposely changed the lesson order around so next week, with the reporter in class, would be an easy lesson, and the more difficult one would be tonight. It wasn't an ideal way to do it, but it beat trying to teach complicated techniques with a reporter hanging around. Besides, the meal for that night was a little unusual, not something she wanted a reporter trying to interpret.

She walked over to the center island. "Tonight's class," she told the men, "is one you'll all need at some point. We're going to prepare a love meal, a meal designed for—"

The ringing of the doorbell blocked out the final words, and Ellie frowned as Sara scurried off to see who it was. She returned in seconds, followed by a man and a woman whom Ellie had never seen before.

"Aunt Ellie?" Sara said. "These people have an appointment with you?"

Ellie focused on the woman behind Sara. She was

dressed impeccably and expensively. Before she could
say a word, the woman spoke up.

"Hello," she said with authority. "I'm Cukie
LaCrosse."

Ellie's eyebrows shot up into her bangs. "Cukie—"

"From the newspaper."

"But—"

"I know, I know." Cukie wiggled long, carefully manicured fingers into the air. "You thought we
were coming next week. Plans change faster than the
weather in this business." Cukie smiled in surprise as
she recognized several of the men in the class. She dis-
pensed some kisses into the air as she greeted them.

Ellie listened to the polished, refined voice and
wondered if Cukie was an imposter. She looked and
sounded like a woman who should be heading a charity drive rather than toting a tape recorder with a
bearded photographer in tow.

"Perhaps if you had called," Ellie began, growing
more anxious with each cheek-kiss Cukie was now
passing out to the men. She wasn't ready to have this
woman here, not now, not tonight, and maybe, from
the looks of her, not ever. "Next week would be much
better for me," she said finally.

Cukie's reply was a smile that displayed perfect
white teeth. She dropped her gold silk jacket on an
empty stool. "But not for me, darling. Something
came up next Wednesday that I can't possibly pass
up. So I am here tonight. And this is Robert, my
photographer, who will take some photos to prove
this little cooking group truly does exist."

The bearded Robert doffed his baseball hat.

Ellie tried again. "I don't think you understand."

"And what is there to understand?" Cukie asked, her brows lifting incredulously.

"I don't want you here toni—" Ellie began, but Cukie's attention had shifted away from her to a point across the room. While Ellie watched, Cukie's narrow face lit with a radiant, red-lipsticked smile. "Peter!" she said, in her perfect voice. "Dear Peter." Her angular body glided across the room.

"Hello, Cukie," Pete said, accepting the kiss she planted firmly on his lips.

"Had I known you were one of the select bachelors playing this little game, I would have approached it all with a tad more enthusiasm. What a treat to see you, darling." Cukie patted his cheek.

Pete accepted the caress nonchalantly.

Ellie stepped in and tried to be heard. "I think it's wonderful that you're doing this story, Ms. LaCrosse, but it really isn't going to work tonight. I need time to prepare—"

"No," Cukie said emphatically, waving one red-tipped finger in the air. "Spontaneity is always best. We want to see things just the way they are, to see what these gentlemen have really learned. Isn't that what this is all about? We don't want you coaching these men for an article, now do we?"

"Coaching—hah!" This came from Tex who, Ellie could see, was regretting his and Estelle's part in calling Cukie. "We're becoming damn fine cooks, Cukie LaCrosse."

"Oh, dear Tex, I'm *sure* you are. Estelle has told me all about your triumphs."

Ellie cringed at the smile that kept coming in different modes with different nuances. Cukie LaCrosse wasn't her favorite kind of person. But it was clear that short of ordering the woman out of her house and probably buying some bad PR to boot, she was stuck with her. And with a roomful of men who were about to have the cooking challenge of their lives. Oh, what the heck. She'd never let challenges deter her before. Cukie LaCrosse was a tiny drop in the challenge bucket. She'd simply ignore the society reporter and get on with things.

"Okay, gentlemen," she said briskly, "enough small talk. Ms. LaCrosse, please make yourself at home. Do what you have to do, and we'll be about our business here. We've a big night ahead of us. On with the aprons, fellows." She grabbed her own white bib from a hook and quickly slipped it over her jeans and T-shirt.

"Don't pay any attention to us," Cukie chirped.

"I don't intend to," Ellie said. She smiled, then she set to work.

"Tonight's class," she began, "is the one I promised you at the beginning of the course. Tonight you'll learn some techniques in preparing the perfect meal for the perfect person. The kind of meal that, in folklore at least, is intended to incite the senses."

Robert the photographer, whom Ellie thought had fallen asleep leaning against the back wall, suddenly straightened and pushed his baseball hat to the back of his head. His sleepy eyes opened wide with interest.

"Tonight," Ellie went on, feeling the familiar rush of adrenaline that teaching induced, "we're going to explore aphrodisiacs and then use some to create the perfect romantic meal." She looked around. The room was eerily quiet except for Cukie's whispered instructions to Robert. Ellie cleared her throat and went on. "Aphrodisiacs, as you may know, are a classification of foods named after the Greek goddess of love, Aphrodite, and believed to stimulate desire."

Tex beamed. "Love potions," he said in a perfect stage whisper. "Estelle will go crazy!" They all laughed, and Ellie went on, explaining that the lore surrounding aphrodisiacs went way back in time.

She pulled out some bowls, talking as she worked. "Aphrodisiacs have quite a history, and some of the ancient recipes were pretty bizarre, things like roasted hummingbird hearts and fried kangaroo testicles."

The men cringed, and Robert began clicking his camera. Ellie concentrated on her cooking lesson.

"But we're interested in good food here, recipes that will satisfy us in a whole bunch of ways. We'll pass up the kangaroos for things like oysters and caviar and rich garlicky and curry sauces. Wonderful foods."

As she set out the eggs and oysters and Cornish hens that they'd be working with, she explained that even potatoes were considered a powerful aphrodisiac in the eighteenth and nineteenth centuries. She could see that Cukie was taking some notes, then poking her microphone in people's faces. Oh well, Ellie wasn't going to let it bother her. She'd done a lot of research for this class and she was going to teach it the way she had planned, from start to finish.

"Since this is a mood thing as well as anything else," she went on, "Pete will pour everyone some wine, we'll put on a Barbra Streisand tape, and loosen up. When you're planning an evening like this, you should make use of all sorts of things—candles, music, nice tablecloths, fresh flowers. Anything that appeals to the senses. And then the meal—" She kissed her fingers and gestured with them, mimicking a grand French chef. "The meal, it will be a sensual delight!"

The wine helped, and soon everyone was in the spirit of things, slicing avocados for the avocado pear salad, mounding caviar on fine crystal plates, and cracking eggs for the curry sauce.

Feeling a tad more generous once things were on a roll, Ellie walked over to Cukie and asked if she needed anything.

Cukie smiled a sugary sweet smile. "Oh, I don't think so. And if I did, I'm not at all sure I would find it here, Ellen." She turned away from Ellie, just in time to see Tex drop a carton of eggs onto the floor. The newly vigilant Robert clicked away.

In retrospect, Ellie decided that that was probably the moment when things fell apart.

With Sara's help, she cleaned up the eggs she could easily reach, ignoring those that had run onto people's shoes. Never once did she lose her cool. Not when Pete's Cornish hen skidded across the work island and she and he both lunged for it at the same time, colliding in midair as they grasped the tiny breast of the fowl. Nor when seventeen oysters slid unceremoniously to the floor an instant before Robert walked by, lost his footing, and then slid with amazing speed across the kitchen floor into the back screen door. Nor when the odor of garlic became so strong that Cukie retreated to the back porch.

Ellie simply poured more wine, helped the men stir their sauces, and insisted that everything was fine.

Finally, blessedly, it was all over.

Blowing kisses to all the men, Cukie left, Robert trailing after her. Ellie waited until she heard the front door close, then she moaned. "She didn't even interview me."

"She said she had everything she needed," Tex said.

"I'll bet she did," Ellie muttered.

Jake patted her arm. "Pay her no mind, Ellie. This was a great class. I loved every minute of it."

The men all seconded that, toasting Ellie with the last drops of wine in their glasses.

"But all the spills—" Ellie murmured.

"We always spill," Pete said.

It was true. They did. So who cared if Cukie saw it? Nobody, that's who.

When the men left, it was with smiles and recipes in hand. The meal, they told her, was fantastic. Memorable. And would make a whole lot of people happy.

"And you," Pete said, speaking so softly into her

ear that the hairs on her neck stood up, "are the best aphrodisiac of all."

When the kitchen was finally empty, Ellie turned to Sara. "I'm absolutely pooped," she said. "You must be too. So we're going to leave the whole mess tonight, you're going home, and I'm going to bed."

Sara's pretty face crumpled. "Oh, Aunt Ellie . . ." she wailed.

Ellie frowned and wrapped her arm around Sara's narrow shoulders. "Hey, Sara, since when does skipping dishes make you sad?"

"Aunt Ellie . . ."

"Sara, hon, what is it? You shouldn't be sad. The evening's over. That's cause for jubilation."

"Aunt Ellie, I have to tell you. We . . . I, like when they left, the lady, I bumped into her, right smack into her—"

"And?"

"And I spilled a whole glass of wine on her silk suit." The words came out in a painful rush.

Ellie held her niece gently and looked into her sad blue eyes. She thought of the expensive gold jacket. "You did, huh."

Sara nodded tearfully.

"White or red?" Ellie asked. She scooped up Sara's sweater and walked her to the front door.

"What?"

"White or red wine?"

Sara cringed. "Red."

"Good," Ellie replied, and with a satisfied grin, she hugged her niece good night.

SIX

For two days Ellie told anyone who would listen that the upcoming article wasn't worth worrying about. She was doing fine; her next cooking session was nearly filled. What damage could Kooky Cukie do? But deep down inside she worried about it like a dog with a bone. She didn't trust Cukie LaCrosse, and she wondered what she would say about Ellie's love meal in a newspaper read by thousands of people.

"Nice friends you have, Webster," she said to Pete when he showed up unexpectedly at her house Saturday evening.

"Cukie isn't much of a friend, Ellie," he said. "We grew up in the same neighborhood, went to the same schools and clubs, know the same people. That's all."

"I don't think she and I would ever even get to the 'not much of a friend' stage."

Pete laughed. "Good. Now, may I come in?"

"My house?"

He looked around. "Yeah. The neighbors weren't home, so I guess you'll have to do." He held out the hand he'd been hiding behind himself and handed her a perfect yellow rose.

"Oh," she said softly. She took the flower, then, suddenly suspicious, quickly looked up. "Why? Do you know what she's written? Is this something to soften the blow? An appeasement?"

"Cukie isn't my responsibility, Ellie," he said. "*I* didn't invite her to the class. It was Tex's voluptuous Estelle and you yourself who did the damage. You wanted the publicity, right?"

"Sure I did." She held open the door, and Pete followed her into the cool shadows of the front hall. "But it wasn't me who gave her such a show. It was all of you, you men with ten thumbs."

She put the rose in a bud vase and set it on a small table in the living room. Pete stood in the doorway, content to watch her movements, the curve of her back, the way she lifted her arms and moved her hands. He wasn't quite sure why he was there. Maybe because he knew Ellie had been a little ruffled by Cukie LaCrosse, even though the men thought it had been a terrific class. Ellie herself had handled it like a pro, but he had seen the look on her face when Cukie had left. With the paper coming out tomorrow, she was probably thinking about it. But it was more than that that had brought him to her door. It was an empty, hollow house with the kids off to New York on a rare visit to see their mother; and the thought of dinner at the club, which held about as much appeal as a tonsillectomy; and it was Ellie herself, who was like a magic magnet, drawing him to her. He had gotten in his Explorer, passed a vendor on the street selling roses, and had ended up at her door.

"Well, no matter," Ellie said, bending low to smell the velvety bud. "Thank you for the flower. It's beautiful."

"Then it's in the right place."

She straightened and looked at him. "But you didn't come all this way to bring me a flower, Pete."

He lifted one shoulder in a small shrug. "Maybe not. But my kids are gone for a couple of days, and I thought, what the hell, maybe Ellie is home and bored, wanting company."

"I see."

"And I said to myself, if she is home, and alone, of course, then I'll remind her how beautiful the sky is at sunset, and maybe, in her slightly skeptical way, she'll say, 'prove it' . . ."

She laughed. "Prove it, Webster."

Pete drove to Grant Park and found a parking place in the lengthening shadows of the Art Institute. "Come on," he said, taking her elbow. "This is a wonderful place to watch the sun go down."

They walked quietly, arm in arm, weaving their way through the traffic and across the expanse of lawn to the huge fountains that stood majestically in the center of the wide green space. Beyond the fountains was the lake, its deep black water gentle that evening, lapping rhythmically against the shore. The sky above the lake had darkened, and toward the west, over the tall buildings of the city—the twin peaks of the Sears Tower, the Tribune building, the old, historic hotels—the sky was fading from light blue to dark, to shades of orange and deep crimson red, and finally the fiery ball disappeared completely and the midnight blue of night began to fill the sky.

A breeze blew in from the lake, but it was only enough to ruffle hair, not enough to chill, and Ellie felt the anxiety of the last few days fade away.

"This was a good idea, Pete. I love it here. The lake has enormous influence over me."

"I would guess it's one of the few things that does."

"You're probably right," she said, then nodded toward a vendor selling hot dogs. "How about it? My treat."

Pete let her go, knowing she wanted it that way, wanted the upper hand, the equality. He'd noticed in class, too, that when she looked at him and the sparks flew, she pulled back and changed directions, planting her feet firmly and moving ahead, confident and in charge.

She returned a few minutes later holding buns filled with fat Polish sausages that were slathered in hot mustard sauce and sauerkraut. Tucked under her arm were two bottles of beer and a thick wad of paper napkins.

"I always wondered what culinary geniuses ate when they had time off," he said, sitting down on a low concrete wall. He bit with relish into one of the plump sausages. Juice squirted out onto the sidewalk.

"Everyone needs one of these every six weeks or so. It keeps the demons away," she said, licking a dollop of mustard from the corner of her mouth.

Pete watched her, mesmerized. When they'd left the house earlier, she had pulled on a loosely woven faded blue sweater, and it fell gently over her breasts and hips. She wore her usual jeans that emphasized her long, elegant legs. Her hair was pulled back into its familiar thick braid. She was totally oblivious to her beauty, he thought, watching the pink tip of her tongue capture the sauce from her lips.

When the tightening in his groin grew to uncomfortable levels, he pulled his gaze away from her and took a long swallow of beer. For the umpteenth time he wondered about it, about the feelings he had when he was with Ellie Livingston. Although he still complained to Rachel, he looked forward to the classes now. He wanted to be there, hearing that slightly throaty voice tell him how to snap his wrist when he beat egg whites and what kind of chicken to buy for grilling. Hell, she might as well be telling him what day to put his garbage out. No matter what she said, it would do the same thing to him—bring him little jolts of unexpected pleasure.

"Tell me something, Webster," she said, jerking him from his thoughts.

"Tell you what?" He took another swallow of beer. They were sitting side by side, their elbows touching every so often as they ate and drank.

"Tell me why you were so pigheaded that night we first met."

"Pigheaded?" He laughed.

"A word my mother always uses when nothing else seems to fit."

He took another swig of beer while he pondered the question. "Okay, why was I so pigheaded? If memory serves me—" Memory, hell. He remembered exactly why he had been in such a mood that night. "I hadn't had an exemplary day, but I didn't think it good manners to back out of the date at the last minute."

"What kind of a bad day?"

"In addition to several other unrelated things at work, I was buying the paper at the newsstand near my office when I saw her on the cover of *Cosmo*." He shook his head. "There she was, smiling at me and God and anyone else who couldn't help staring at the gorgeous cover gal with the perfect breasts that were spilling out of the slinky red dress."

"Who—?"

"My children's mother," he said tersely.

Ellie felt the emotion surround her. There was real pain in Pete's voice. She touched his arm. "I'm sorry, Pete. What a crummy thing for the kids, to have their friends, their friends' parents, see that."

He looked at her in surprise, then half-smiled. "That's not the response I usually get. A lot of people who saw the magazine kidded me, asked how I could possibly have let someone like her—gorgeous, sexy, witty—get away. Not many people thought of my children, what it would be like for them to have people see their mom that way, nearly naked on a magazine cover. And that's the part that made me ready to spit nails that night. And then you were so damn beautiful, too, and that made it worse."

Questions began to pile up in Ellie's mind, but she wasn't sure if this was the time to ask them. She tucked them away and instead playfully nudged Pete in the side. "All you had to do was ask, Pete. I would have told you right off I didn't own a single slinky red dress. And I don't think my breasts have ever spilled out of anything. Except maybe once, when I was in seventh grade and my friend Janice and I went to Marshall Field's to buy our first bras. It was cool to spill then."

"I shoulda asked," Pete said, grinning. He felt a pleasant shift inside himself, a comfortable slide of emotion. Mentioning Elaine hadn't brought with it the usual spurt of anger. Instead he felt a nice connection to this unlikely woman sitting next to him. And with the next swig of beer he admitted that what he wanted to do was not be angry at something that had happened in the past, but enjoy the present. What he wanted to do was to wrap an arm around this woman beside him. He looked over at her and touched her cheek. "I don't think knowing that about you would have saved the evening, though. I was pretty impervious to any kind of rescue."

"Probably not." Ellie took a last bite of her Polish sausage and washed it down with a long swallow of beer. She stretched her legs out in front of her. "We definitely weren't charmed by each other."

"And now?"

"Now?"

A crumb from the hot dog bun was resting in the corner of her mouth. Pete watched it as her lips opened, then closed on the single word.

"Yeah," he said. "What do you think of me now?" Without a lot of thought, but with a great deal of instinct, he set his beer can at his feet, then wrapped his fingers around Ellie's upper arms, turning her toward him. As she looked up her eyes filled with a swirl of emotion that fueled him. He pulled her close and lowered his head until his lips closed over hers.

Ellie responded instantly, parting her lips and tasting the sweet moistness of his mouth. The teasing ripples of desire that began in her center fanned out in all directions and spread like wildfire, coursing through her entire body, her legs, her stomach, up through her breasts. And still he kissed her, his tongue probing, touching her own as he plunged in to explore the cave of her mouth.

It was Pete who finally pulled away. Ellie sat immobile. The bracing lake air washed over her heated face. The coolness was an intrusion, pulling her away from the sweet, wonderful sensations of Pete's kiss. She hadn't wanted him to stop.

He brushed a loose strand of hair behind her ear. "I don't know, but I'd say we have it in us to charm each other. That was sort of charming, don't you think?" He tipped her chin up so he could see her eyes.

" 'Charming' isn't the word that comes to mind," she managed to say, her voice ragged.

"Good," he said, then wrapped his arm around her and turned her sideways. "Look."

Several yards beyond the low wall, people had gathered around the fountains. They were lighting up against the black sky in a brilliant explosion of color, lifting majestically into the air and falling back down in waves of blue, then pink, then dazzling, gleaming greens.

Pete and Ellie sat together, shoulders touching as they watched the mesmerizing light-and-water show. In the distance, like lovely background music, rose the oohs and ahs of the crowd, and Pete and Ellie slipped into the wonderment of it all. The puzzling, sensual connection was growing slowly between them, knitting them together as surely as the colored waters of the fountain that flowed into one another until there was no color left at all.

Ellie shivered and allowed Pete's arms to surround her in an effort to ward off the chill. The cold feeling remained, though, deep down inside her. Woven into it was a cautious voice—Franny would say it was her guardian angel, whom she had long ago named Joe— reminding her that this wasn't in her present plan. Not a man. And not a man like Pete.

"And why not a man like Pete?" Fran demanded the next morning when she called and pulled Ellie from the deep cushiony cavern of sleep.

"Because he's not just for fun," Ellie murmured, swinging her feet to the floor beside the bed. "He's—

he's different, Franny. Seeing him is too complicated, I think. It's more than just an evening out."

Fran repeated her sister's words out loud, then sighed. "Ellie, for once in your life, forget about the future, about business, about tomorrow. Go with your feelings for a change. Damn the consequences. Just enjoy life."

Ellie pondered that while she fished beneath her bed for her slippers. "I *do* enjoy life, Fran."

"You know what I mean."

"You mean I need a man to enjoy life. Not true. Who needs a man when she can create soufflés to die for and give birth to a wonderful business all by herself?"

"Balderdash."

Ellie laughed. The laughter brushed away the last fogginess of sleep. And then it hit Ellie. "Yikes!" she yelled, directly into the phone.

On the other end, Fran rubbed her ear. "Yikes, what?"

"It's Sunday, Fran." Ellie's voice dropped to barely a whisper. "Judgment day."

"The article. I almost forgot."

Without another word, the two sisters hung up and raced for the thick roll of Sunday newspaper sitting on their respective front stoops.

When Ellie, her thin nightgown whipping against her bare legs, stepped out onto the porch, her pathway to the paper was blocked by a pair of jeans and a yellow knit shirt. Inside of them was Pete Webster. Stuck under his arm was a fat newspaper.

"Pete," she whispered.

Pete stared. Her hair, thick and loose and glorious, floated around her head like a cloud. Her nightgown was nearly transparent, a wisp of washed cotton falling over her body like a light veil. Her feet were bare, her face free of makeup. He swallowed hard around the lump in his throat and willed other parts of him to calm down as well. With great concentration he forced a smile to his face. "Morning, Ellie."

"What . . . what—"

"I picked the paper up on my way back from running. Thought I'd bring you a copy in case . . ."

"I . . . we . . ." Ellie groped for words. She knew how she must look, but this was her house, after all, her terrain, and she wouldn't act flustered. She looked down at the stoop and took a deep breath. When she spoke, her voice was bright and cheery. "How nice of you. I do get the paper, though. See?" She pointed to it on the top step.

Pete glanced at it, then back to her. "But does yours come with coffee?" He held up a sack showing the outline of two Styrofoam cups. "McDonald's special."

Ellie brushed her hair back over her shoulder, wishing she'd had the good sense to grab her robe. "This could become a habit, Webster," she said lightly. "Opening up my front door and finding you on the step."

"But easily broken. You could use your back door."

"I guess I could." She took a deep breath. "Well, okay, come on in. The coffee does smell good." For a minute she forgot the article. The sight of Pete with the morning light behind him, smelling as though he had just stepped out of the shower, had taken over most of her senses. The one she counted on, *common* sense, had been lost in the shuffle.

"Did you bring any food?" she asked over her shoulder as he followed her down the hall.

"No."

"I'm starving. I'll whip up something to go with the coffee."

There, she thought. How was that for acting natural? They were in the kitchen now, and she grabbed a cardigan sweater from a hook. After pulling it on, she turned to him, smiled, and motioned toward one of the stools. "You sit. I'll cook."

"Ellie—" he began.

Again, she remembered. It all came back in a giant rush that knocked the air out of her lungs. She pressed her hands down on the counter. "The article! This time that's really it; that's why you're here. Damage control."

"No. It'll be fine, Ellie. It's light, a humorous slant. Come on, let's read it—get it over with—before you fuss around in here."

"It's fine?" she said weakly.

"Well, sure. My twin sister thought it was hilarious."

"Twin sister! No wonder you always remember her birthday. That negates that one good quality, Webster. It's cheating. You're going to have to come up with another—" She realized she was babbling.

Avoiding the issue. She wanted to babble some more, but Peter wasn't listening.

He was opening the magazine, turning it to the middle article. "You're a centerfold," he told her. He smoothed it out flat on the island so they could read it together. Ellie approached cautiously. Standing beside him, she slowly read the headline and subhead. Her pained groan filled the room as she slumped onto a stool and read it a second time:

COOKING WITH ELLIE IS A SENSUAL ROMP
Aphrodite in an Apron

SEVEN

With slow, deliberate movements, Ellie walked over to the counter and got herself a cup of strong coffee. Then she walked back to where Pete sat with the newspaper. She perched on the stool next to him and forced herself to read every single Cukie-written word.

The article was laced with Robert's pictures, and in the very center, spanning both sides of the page, was one of her, Ellie Livingston, in Pete Webster's arms as they grabbed for a wayward Cornish hen. The caption read: *Teacher and student keep a-breast of things*.

Finally, after she had read the entire article, Ellie rose from the stool and wandered off to the sink to pour herself a glass of cold water. She drank it slowly, looking out the open window, and she wondered vaguely if she had remembered to put bird feed out the day before. Several robins were perched on the outside sill and looked at her quizzically.

As Pete watched her, her body a sensuous blend of curves as she leaned against the sink, he was aware, once again, of how quickly the focus of the here and now blurred when he was with her. Words became fuzzy and were replaced by a thrumming, a sensation that affected the rhythm of his life. He was so entranced with looking at her, he barely heard her when she spoke.

"Don't they have editors at that paper? How could *anyone* have let that story pass?" She turned to look at him. "Pete? Do you hear me?"

He forced himself to focus. "It's not that bad an article, Ellie."

"Not bad?" Her cheeks flamed. "It makes my cooking course sound like a preschool for the Kinsey Sex Institute."

"People know Cukie. She writes a lot of stuff on the society page, and readers will interpret the article in that light. They know her, know how she exaggerates and pokes fun."

"No, everyone *doesn't* know Cukie, Pete. You do, and a certain segment of society might, but I, for example, had never heard of Cukie LaCrosse before. For all I might think, she's an astute recorder of life, a Studs Terkel, a . . . a—"

"Oh, come on, Ellie. What does it matter anyway? It's just an article."

"Just an article? And *you*, Mr. Webster, claim to be in advertising?" As she gripped the edge of the sink, it dawned on Ellie what Pete was saying, and the familiar rush of anger set in. It wasn't the article that didn't matter, it was the course itself that didn't matter. To Pete this was not a big deal, not Cukie, not what she said in her article, and most of all, not the cooking course. She glared at him. "It matters a lot, Pete. This is my business we're talking about here. *My* business, and the kind of PR it's getting. Of *course* it matters."

"Ellie, I—" He stood up, but she interrupted him with a rush of words and a wave of her hands.

"To you it may be a hobby, but to me it's a career. This is important to me, Webster, and frankly I don't like it that some bored society woman, with all her sexual innuendos, her silly rattling on, is messing with my carefully planned course. She knows nothing—"

"Hey—" Pete walked over to her, drawn by the power of her emotion. He held her arms against her sides. She seemed as fragile as the tea rose he had brought over the day before. "I didn't mean that, Ellie," he said quietly. "You're overreacting. Sure these courses are important to you. What's not important is one damn article. Did you notice what else is in the paper today?"

She shook her head.

"The Cubs just won their twentieth game in a row, that's what," he said. "Twenty games, El. In a row. And the paper is full of special interviews and spectacular color shots. That's what the city is talking about today, not Cukie's article."

"And that's supposed to make me feel good? You don't get it, do you, Pete?" She wiggled free of his hold.

"On some level here," he said slowly, "we're not

communicating very well." He could feel the emotional sparks flying all around them. Hell, he was trying to make her feel better, but everything he said seemed to fuel the fire in her.

"That's right, we're not!" she snapped. "This cooking course isn't a hobby or a way to keep me from being bored, Pete. It's a livelihood, a career, a—"

She brushed past him, and for an instant, through the thin gown, he felt the light pressure of her breasts on his arm. He swallowed hard but stayed in place as she walked across the kitchen and pulled a package of milk chocolate squares from the cupboard. Next came the eggs and butter from the refrigerator, all lined up carefully on the island. The bowls and mixing tools came next.

Pete watched the flashes of fierce determination light up her face as she worked. "What are you doing?" he finally asked.

She spun around and stared at him as if he had completely lost his mind. "What am I doing?" she repeated slowly.

He nodded.

She answered him with forced patience, the way an overworked teacher would explain a math problem for the sixth time to an inattentive student.

"What I am doing, Webster, is baking. I'm going to make brownies and cookies and chocolate cake. And while I cook, I will slowly but surely rid myself of every iota of frustration that your dear friend Cukie LaCrosse has brought into my life." She brushed a wisp of hair from her cheek and tipped up her chin, her eyes blazing as they locked with his. Her look dared him to challenge her.

Pete had no intention of challenging her. All he could think of at that moment was the remarkable power of lust. It must be the combination of Ellie and chocolate, he thought—an overpowering aphrodisiac if ever there was one. She stood a few feet from him in her bare feet, her hair still tousled from sleep, and sunlight streaming through her thin nightgown. Her sensuality was so incredibly intense, he knew there was only one course of action for him that he could live with, only one option that wouldn't have consequences Ellie would make him regret.

So he did what he had to do. He gritted his teeth, turned slowly, and walked out of the kitchen, down the hall, and out the front door. Although he didn't look back, he carried with him the image of Ellie's slender body outlined in bold, naked detail by the morning sunlight, and her beautiful face, fresh as the morning dew.

Ellie didn't look up until the last moment, just in time to see a flash of Pete's back before he disappeared from sight. She had felt it, too, the power of the attraction between them, and it had left her momentarily stunned. Here she was, furious about all sorts of things, and her body was quivering like a bride's on her wedding night.

She brushed the newspaper aside and headed up the back steps to the shower. She'd make it as cold as she could stand it. The brownies would have to wait.

When she stepped out of the bathroom a while

later, the phone was ringing. She hurried into the bedroom, leaving small puddles of water in her wake.

"Hello?" she said breathlessly, wondering if it would be a student backing out of a future class. Would they do that on a Sunday? But it was Fran, so excited that Ellie could barely make out her words.

"Slow down, Fran," she said. She pulled the towel around her and sat on the side of the bed. "Now start over, slowly this time."

"We need to send Cukie LaCrosse a dozen roses!" Fran said.

"The thorns maybe. Not a bad idea," Ellie said.

"No, Ellie! You could not have bought this kind of publicity. It's fantastic. Cukie put our reservation number in the article, and I've already received more than a dozen phone calls—and it's Sunday morning, for heaven sakes!"

"Franny," Ellie said slowly, "are you pregnant again?"

Fran laughed. "This time, Ellie, you're the one having the baby. And it's growing fast! It seems everyone and his brother are fighting to get in your class. It's *the* thing to give boyfriends and lovers and sons and even husbands! Everyone wants in, El. I raised the price, and—"

"You what?"

"Yup, absolutely. You're always preaching about it, so I did it. Something about supply and demand. I told everyone the first course had been at a special rate, but I didn't even need to explain. No one balked at the cost."

"That's ridiculous," Ellie said, shaking her head. She was unable to take it all in, so she concentrated on a peripheral, unconnected fact. "What kind of a world is it when people are homeless and hungry and others are paying a small fortune for a *cooking* course!"

"Ellie, shhh. This is your business we're talking about. But I agree. It is a little crazy."

"We're going to need to set up something to benefit charity, Fran. Leftover food, maybe a cookathon for the homeless—" Her mind was racing from thought to thought, the earlier frustration of the morning lying in lovely shreds at her feet. Her heart began to pump faster.

"There you go. But anyway, sweetums, it looks like 'For Men Only' will play in Peoria. I need to hang up to free the line."

"Wait. Fran—"

"What, El?"

"What about the Cubs?"

"Baby bears?"

"No, the other ones. Did you read about the Cubs today?"

Fran laughed. "Of course not. Are you all right, El? Why would I do that?"

Ellie smiled into the phone. "Who knows?" she said, and hung up.

By Monday Fran had filled up the next cooking course and added a second one on another night to take care of the overflow. She had also set Ellie up for two more interviews and a radio spot. When she called Ellie with the good news, she hit her up for a raise.

Ellie laughed gleefully, agreed instantly, and invited the entire family over for a celebration dinner. "But wait a few days," she said, "until I can get things under control."

Her mother accepted the invitation after carefully voicing one concern. "I would hope, Eleanor," she said, "that none of the gentlemen students are cooking. . . ." Ellie assured her that she was safe, that it would be Ellie in the kitchen and no one else.

Then she called her favorite florist and ordered a huge bouquet of flowers to be delivered to Tex and Estelle. They were the ones, after all, who had gotten Cukie to write the article. To Cukie, as an afterthought, she sent a cactus. Ellie had nearly hung up the phone when she paused, then hurriedly told the salesperson to add a third delivery to the order. She explained the kinds of flowers to put in the arrangement, then gave Pete Webster's name and address from her class roster. The card read: *Hooray for the Cubs.*

Pete didn't call Ellie immediately. He wanted to simply enjoy the gesture for a while. In all his thirty-six years no one had ever sent him flowers before. If asked, he would have said he wouldn't *want* someone to send him flowers. But here he was, sitting in front of an arrangement of yellow daisies and purple iris and a riot of wildflowers that he couldn't name, looking at them as if they were a valuable treasure entrusted to his care.

Sweet ripples of pleasure coursed through him when he smelled them, then he smiled in a way he couldn't remember smiling for a long, long time.

The kids were still in New York for their once-a-year visit with Elaine. Pete hated for them to miss school, but he knew it was important for them to spend time with their mother. Rachel and Paul were on a trip, too, so he could enjoy the sensations privately, without explanation to anyone. He could simply sit there in his den and smile the whole night if he felt like it.

When he did call Ellie, he got an answering machine, informing him that "For Men Only" was full until January, at which time new classes would be formed. If interested, he could leave his name and phone number.

January. Incredible. She was going to make it. The thought tugged at him, unsettling somehow. But that was silly. He wanted her to succeed. They all did, the whole class. In just a few short weeks all the men, even a die-hard male chauvinist who sat in the back and leered at Ellie continuously, had fallen slightly in love with the bright, beautiful cooking instructor who was actually teaching them to cook.

When he finally got hold of Ellie a day later, calling from his office when he had a free minute, she was out of breath and her hello was carried on a breathy sound.

"I like the way you breathe," he said.

"Yeah, people tell me that all the time." Ellie smiled on her end. She'd wondered earlier why he hadn't called. After telling herself there was no reason he should call, she had gone into the kitchen and baked a loaf of bread.

"The Cubs lost today," he said.

"Too bad."

"But the flowers are great, no matter."

"Good."

"Thanks."

"You're welcome."

Damn, Pete thought, was he sixteen or thirty-six? Why couldn't he think of anything to say? And then he knew why. It was because the words that flooded his mind were dangerous ones: *I've been thinking of you, Ellie, a lot. I want to be with you. I want to learn more from you than how to make a soufflé. I—*

"Pete, are you still there?"

"Yeah."

"Are your kids back yet?"

"No."

"I'm cooking a dinner for my family tonight. Would you like to join us?"

"Your family?"

"Yes. A mother, sisters and brothers. Husbands and wives. Kids. That kind."

"Oh. Well, I don't think—"

"I understand if you have other plans. But there'll be lots of food. It's a celebration. Things are going so well, Pete. We have a waiting list and calls from the media for interviews. And since you're alone, I thought you might like to join us, help us celebrate."

Pete nodded. It was lonely without the kids. He wanted to see Ellie; he wanted to be with her. Hell, he wanted to touch her, to hold her, to do a whole lot of things, but they wouldn't exactly fit into a family dinner.

"This isn't a 'come home to meet my family' kind of invitation," she went on. "The Livingstons have always taken in strays, and since you're without family for a few days . . ."

"I'm a stray, huh?"

"Sort of."

"Well, that's different, then."

"Come about seven."

He was smiling when he hung up, but meeting Ellie's family didn't have a thing to do with it.

"You're early," Ellie said, opening the door to let Pete in.

"I came right from work. No sense in fighting my way out to the suburbs just to turn around and come back."

"And here I thought it was because you couldn't wait another minute to see me." She grinned up at him, running her hands down the sides of her apron.

"Well, that too." He followed her into the dining room, where she was arranging silverware on an enormous table.

"My family takes up a lot of room," she explained, "and you never know who'll bring extras."

"When I was a kid, my family ate at a table three times as large as this, and there were only four of us."

Ellie's eyebrows lifted. "How could you talk to each other? How could you elbow someone if you wanted the ketchup? How awful!"

Her description was apt, Pete mused. He had always hated family meals. Maids hovered and his father pontificated and his mother fussed. Training, she had called it when they were young. Mealtimes were opportunities to develop social graces. He suspected they were something totally different for Ellie's family.

"Do you see your family much, Pete?"

"I see my sister, Rachel, all the time, sometimes more than I want to," he added, but the affection in his voice was clear. "Rachel's great. You'd like her."

"They say twins have a sixth sense about each other, that they're tuned in to each other in a special way. That must be nice."

"Usually it is. Sometimes Rachel tunes in a little too much, but I love her just the same."

"And your parents?"

"My parents have homes all over the world, and they move around a lot, depending on the weather. It's fall, so they're probably on their way to the house in the Cayman Islands. They check in with Rach and me occasionally."

Ellie couldn't quite read his tone. There was respect there, but although she tried hard to hear it, not much else. She wanted to ask him more, but the sound of footsteps at the back door told her this wasn't the time. An instant later three youngsters tumbled into the kitchen, followed by several of Ellie's brothers and sisters. In minutes her house was humming with voices and crowded with hugs and kisses.

Introductions were hastily made, then Fran took over, taking Pete by the arm and rehashing with much laughter Ellie's first date with him. Ellie watched the two of them out of the corner of her eye, her arms full of baby as she cuddled a six-month-old niece. Fran was not one to be trusted in matters of the heart, and she had made it crystal clear to Ellie that she liked what she knew of Pete Webster. "Harvey," Ellie whispered to Fran's husband, "watch those two. Don't let Fran get carried away."

Harvey grinned as he piled two six-packs of beer into Ellie's refrigerator. "Aw, El, don't deprive her. She gets such a kick out of matchmaking."

"Well, she can concentrate on Danny. I don't want her services."

"And I don't *need* them," Danny said, appearing at her side with a beautiful young woman. Danny was blond and handsome and, as the baby of the Livingston clan, had been spoiled for twenty-two years by his brothers and sisters. Danny nodded toward Pete. "I like him, Ellie."

"You don't have to like him, Danny. He's not a prospect."

Danny took a swig of his beer and looked at Pete again. He was standing next to their mother, towering over her. "Look at him over there with Ma. He's passing the first test, El."

"Danny, stop it, he's only here because his kids are out of town. He doesn't need to pass the test!" She glanced over at the laughing group herself and pulled her brows together. Pete was holding Fran's daughter Claire, a three-year-old bundle of mischief. Claire was giggling as Pete helped her climb around his neck to position herself on his shoulders for a ride. Ellie groaned.

"Told you," Danny said. "Whatever your intentions, Ellie, he's making a hit over there."

"I think it's time to eat," Ellie said. She banged a metal spoon against a pot, and the ringing echoed through the kitchen, hushing the Livingston clan. "Okay, lovies," she called. "Time for chow, but first a big thank-you to all of you for helping me set my cooking business in motion."

She blinked rapidly to hold back unexpected tears as she smiled at her family.

"I love you all," she said, and the catch in her voice was drowned out by a chorus of "Hear, hears" and exclamations of congratulations.

"Okay, so sit. All of you," she said quickly, ducking her head to hide the tear rolling down her cheek.

Everyone crowded into the dining room, and as if by tacit agreement, they left the chair on one side of Pete empty. When Ellie finally went to sit down, there was only one possibility.

"Hi," she said softly to Pete as she settled herself on the folding chair. "Are you okay?" Laughter and voices and the clattering of dishes rose up around them.

"Sure. Your family is great, Ellie. Your mom was a little nervous when I was introduced. I think she thought I was student help, but once she was convinced I didn't have anything to do with the meal, we became fast friends."

"Ma likes everyone," Ellie said quickly.

"I knew there was a reason."

"I didn't mean—"

"Shhh. Try this. It's great food. The chef must be something special." Pete filled his mouth with a heaping forkful of ratatouille.

It was the last time she got a chance to talk alone with him. Everyone wanted a piece of Pete, and his attention was stretched from her brother Danny, who discovered Pete liked coaching kids' basketball games just as he did, to elderly Aunt Eleanor, after whom Ellie was named and who was determined to discover Pete's intentions.

"He's in my cooking class, Aunt Ella," Ellie tried to explain in a voice loud enough for Ella to hear. But Aunt Ella was selective in her hearing and was more interested in exploring how old Pete was, the state of his health, where he lived, and what his plans were for the next fifty years.

Pete handled it all without a hitch, listening politely to family stories, helping Aunt Ella up from her chair when she had to leave the table, letting Claire sit on his lap while they all downed huge pieces of Ellie's carrot cake. Ellie kept sneaking glances at him, wondering when he'd show some relative-fatigue, but she never saw it.

It was a weeknight—school and work the next day—and Ellie's large family was quick to bundle up leftovers and children and move on into the night when the meal was finished. Pete assured several family members that he'd handle the dishes—Ellie had taught him how—and they should go along and put their kids to bed.

Ellie saw his words settle down around her sisters as if he were wrapping them in cashmere coats—and she saw the look they gave him in return, the kind of look reserved for knights in shining armor. Suddenly she wished he'd say something vulgar or obscene, anything to protect her from the fallout of the impression he was making on them. She'd hear about it for the next year, hear about that wonderful man who'd stayed to do the dishes, who'd jostled little Claire on his knee, who'd thrown a ball to Georgie and Kevin to keep them from pulling each other's hair.

Ellie knew, though, what was making Pete stay. It was the same thing that woke her up in the middle of the night and sent her scurrying for cold showers. Unbridled desire, that's what it was. It lay there between them like smoldering coals, a cruel trick of nature pulling them together.

"Pete, I'll do these in the morning," she said when the door had closed behind the last of her family. "It was nice of you to offer, but it's not a big deal."

"I want to help. I liked being here tonight, and I want to thank you by doing the dishes."

She looked at him out of the corner of her eye. "That's it?"

"You want more?" He scratched his head. "Okay, I suppose I could do the wash, scrub a floor maybe. Haven't done much of that, but I could probably figure it out. The meal *was* fantastic. . . ."

She leaned against the counter and shook her head. "Pete, I don't figure you. I think I know what's going on, and then you say something like that, and—" She stopped, sighed, and poured two mugs full of hot coffee. "Let's look at the stars for a while. They're not always out there. Dirty dishes are forever with us."

"You're the boss," Pete said, and held open the screen door so they could step out into the crisp September night. "Nice." He breathed in deeply. "Even the sky over Chicago is clear tonight. It must be an omen."

Ellie sat down on the top step of her tiny back porch, and he slid down beside her, stretching his legs out beyond the steps. His thigh rubbed gently against her cotton skirt, a pleasant soothing touch that she was reluctant to stop by moving over. "Pete, I have to tell you, you surprise me."

"Good. Surprises are good for the soul, Ellie." His head was back, his eyes focused on the stars above.

"Don't you want to know why?"

"I know why. Because I wasn't the bumbling, uncomfortable fool you expected me to be in the middle of all your relatives tonight. But you underestimate people, Ellie. That's a bad habit you ought to toss out."

"Maybe I should," she murmured.

"Our upbringings were definitely light years apart, El, but I like what went on here tonight. I always resented not having people around to joke and hug and nudge one another. I like grabbing beers from the refrigerator instead of having a maid bring one on a silver platter. I like having kids and adults messing around together. It's the kind of family life I want *my* kids to have."

"Traditional."

"I guess, yes."

"And do they?"

"Not yet, not completely. But I work at it. They didn't have a very conventional start, so it may take a while."

"Why did their mother leave, Pete?" she asked softly.

He pointed out Cassiopeia's five brightest stars—its chair—to Ellie. Then he lowered his eyes and said quietly, "Elaine found she didn't much like being a mother. She didn't like the day-to-day sorts of things, and I didn't want a nanny or nursemaid around my house. Occasional help, okay, but raising the kids is the parents' job, no one else's."

Ellie heard the fierceness creep into his voice. She leaned into his strong body, and he went on.

"It wasn't just her philosophy of parenting that caused the rift, although everything sort of fit together. Elaine is breathtakingly beautiful. She didn't have a whole lot growing up, and she always wanted to 'be someone,' as she put it, on her own. She wanted to use her beauty to make her famous. And she has," he added softly.

"So she left you with the children?"

"That was a mutual agreement. I wanted them, and they didn't fit into her plans comfortably. So there was no battle. The kids are my life. They're great."

Ellie smiled in the darkness. "I don't doubt that. They have a pretty nice dad."

"He has his moments."

"That's true."

Pete laughed.

"You have your hands full," she said finally.

"That's right."

"Will you marry again?"

"Depends."

She accepted his answer without further questioning. It made sense that he probably would marry again, with a woman who would fit into the world he wanted for his children. A world not unlike Franny's, Ellie thought. A world far apart from her own.

"Enough about domestic issues," he said. "I'm not sure that's of much interest to you."

She wondered briefly if he had read her mind. "No, not now."

"This business means a great deal to you?"

"Yes. I've always been like this, even as a kid. It was *my* lemonade stand that survived the neighborhood glut, mine that added cookies and take-out orders to people who couldn't get out of their houses. And it was mine that ended up being franchised." She tipped her chin up, grinning. "The secret, Pete, is fresh lemons and a touch of rind." She laughed out loud. "I drove my parents crazy."

"Do you still?"

"Oh, since my father died a few years ago, Ma has gotten a little more cantankerous about my not being married. I think it's just that security thing, knowing I'll have someone. You know."

Pete didn't know, at least not from the point of view she was talking about. But he knew from a parent's point of view, knew keenly what he wanted for his own children. Security, although not at the top of the list, was certainly there.

"Oh, look!" she said, and he lifted his eyes just in time to see a streak of light across the sky.

Ellie squeezed her eyes shut. He watched her, saw the intensity in her striking face, and smiled.

Finally her eyes opened and she looked at him suspiciously. "You didn't wish, did you?"

"Nope. I believe you have to work for what you want. Wishing isn't worth a tinker's damn."

"Oh, I believe in working to make your goals come true, too, but a little magic in one's life never hurts, either."

He rubbed the side of her neck gently with his thumb, an automatic gesture stimulated purely by the way she made him feel. Maybe there was something to this magical business, he mused. He'd have to think about it.

Beside him Ellie tuned in to the sensations created by his touch. They were flowing in a lovely way down from the point of contact, across her shoulders, along her arms, like soft, warm raindrops in the spring. His touch was light, rhythmic, soothing. When the erratic beats of her heart interrupted her meandering thoughts, she realized it wasn't exactly soothing anymore. Something else was coming into play here.

Pete felt the tension in her body, first in her leg that lined up against his own, then in her shoulders and neck. She didn't pull away, though.

"You know, Ellie," he said carefully, "we're wearing each other out trying to avoid this kind of contact. But there's something bigger than us at work here, I think."

"Maybe," she said, and lifted her head to look into his eyes.

With slow, slightly shaky movements, she raised her palm to his cheek and sighed, a soft, sensual sound. Then she lifted her head an inch higher, opened her mouth, and kissed him. Time stopped until she finally pulled away. She took a deep breath and looked up at him. When she spoke, her voice was ragged. "I believe . . . sometimes . . . it's better . . . you know . . . to give in. To feelings. You know . . . ?"

He nodded, his arm wrapping around her and pulling her to him. "Prevents heart attacks," he murmured against her cheek.

"Ummm," she said, her voice a puff of warm air against his face. "You understand . . ."

"Absolutely. Purely a preventive medicinal thing here."

"Purely . . ."

His lips claimed hers again, more hungry this time,

probing, exploring, and savoring the wonderful taste of her. As she eagerly returned his kisses, he slipped his hand beneath the loose tail of her blouse. Her skin, smooth as silk, was cool to his touch, then warm as he flattened his palm against her lower back.

The cool air blew softly around her head, but Ellie felt only heat, all different kinds of heat—the searing imprint of Pete's hand on her back, the fiery blood coursing through her veins, the feverish tingle on her lips.

His fingers moved on her back, up over the delicate curve of her shoulder blades. His other hand slid slowly beneath the front of her blouse and stroked the baby-soft skin of her belly.

Ellie didn't move. It felt too good. Surely she was allowed these feelings now and again, these incredibly marvelous jolts of pleasure. She clung to him as his fingers explored her skin, climbing upward until he cupped one breast in his hand and began to stroke it, his thumb rubbing her nipple in a maddening rhythm. "Oh, Pete," she murmured.

" 'Oh Pete' what?" he asked, dropping tiny kisses along her nose.

"Oh, Pete, I think there's another good quality in all this . . . somewhere—" She could barely breathe.

"Feels good to me," he said, whispering into the side of her neck.

Tiny goose bumps all along her neck leapt to life to meet his words. She wove her fingers through his hair, clinging to him, wanting the night to stand still for her so she could breathe in all that was sweet and delicious about him, so she could give in to the sensations swirling inside of her without having to think about tomorrow.

"Aunt Ellie?"

Ellie jerked away from Pete as if he'd pushed her. Frantically she smoothed her wrinkled blouse and flattened her mussed hair. Finally she turned in the dark, back toward the voice coming from the well-lit kitchen. Sara's silhouette, outlined clearly behind the screen door, was still. "Sara?" she said softly.

"Oh, it *is* you, Aunt El. You scared me."

Scared *you?* Ellie thought, pressing one hand against her rapidly beating heart.

"Hi, Sara," Pete said. "What's up?"

"Oh, Pete!" Sara said cheerfully. "It's you too. I thought so. I came over to get a book I left here, and the phone was ringing, so I answered it. It's for you."

"Me?" Pete forced himself to focus, then got up from the steps, pulling Ellie after him. "Strange. No one knows I'm here."

"It's some lady."

Ellie glanced at him. She could feel the ground beneath her feet, and that was a good sign. And it was sturdy, flat, not moving. She could handle this. "I suggest we go inside," she said in a calm, level voice.

"Aunt Ellie, you sound strange," Sara said, peering out into the darkness. "Are you okay?"

Ellie smiled brightly as she opened the door. "I'm fine, Sara. We were getting some fresh air . . . to cool us off—"

"To wake us up," Pete said hastily. "So we could do the dishes without falling asleep."

"Oh," said Sara, frowning at the two adults in front of her. "Maybe you better get the phone, though, before the lady hangs up. She seemed anxious to talk to you."

Pete nodded as he and Ellie walked into the kitchen, and he quickly picked up the dangling receiver of the wall phone.

Sara grabbed the left-behind history book from the kitchen counter. "Thanks, Aunt El. Gotta go. Dad's in the car." She threw Ellie a kiss, then disappeared down the front hall.

Ellie watched her until she couldn't see her anymore, then slowly turned back toward Pete. He was speaking in low tones, his voice tight, no longer husky with desire.

She saw his thick, well-shaped brows pull together as he listened, a look of worry washing across his face. "When?" he asked. Then, "Thanks, Rachel. I'll be there."

After he hung up, he stood with his back to Ellie for a minute, his eyes searching for something out in the blackness of the night.

"Is everything okay?" she asked at last.

"Fine," he said, turning toward her. He raked his fingers through his hair, forced a half-smile, and shrugged. "But I have to leave you with this mess, El."

For a moment she wasn't sure what he meant. Then she realized he was talking about the dirty pots and pans, not about the mess inside her.

"That was my sister," he went on. "Don't know what possessed her to call me here, but she did. It's her sixth sense, I guess. Anyway, it seems my kids are about to touch down at O'Hare Airport. Elaine had a photo shoot in Majorca that she couldn't pass up, so she put the kids on the plane and sent them home. Easy come, easy go."

For a long time after he left, Ellie stood at the kitchen door and looked out into the velvety star-studded sky. Cassiopeia's chair was still there, its five brightest stars winking in the black night. But it wasn't stars that she saw. What she saw instead was the shadow of a plane, a plane that was lowering its landing gear, maybe right that very minute, preparing for a landing that would bring Pete's kids to him, and away from a mother who didn't have time for them.

EIGHT

It was the first cooking class Pete had missed.

Lucy's chicken pox, however, which popped out the day after she came back from seeing her mother in New York, was making her miserable. He left a message for Ellie on her answering machine, called a neighbor to stay with the kids, then rushed to the store for Benadryl and ginger ale.

When he returned, Lucy, nearly invisible in her fluffy pink robe, was huddled like a ball of fur at the end of the couch in the family room with the phone pressed to her ear. Nearby, P.J. was glued to the television, watching the final minutes of a Lakers game.

"Who's on the phone?" Pete asked P.J.

The boy, dark haired and freckled, shrugged, reluctant to tear himself away from the last shots.

Pete looked at Lucy. Her face was already covered with dozens of small raised pocks, and they were still popping out. Finally Lucy looked up at him and smiled.

"Who is it?" he whispered. Could it be Elaine? She rarely called from New York; calling from Majorca would be a miracle.

Without moving the phone, Lucy said, "It's Ellie, Daddy," as if the two of them were frequent phone pals.

"Ellie?"

"She said she's your friend. She's telling me about the chick and paws."

"Oh." Pete glanced at his watch. It was nine o'clock, the middle of class. Besides the fact that Ellie had never met Lucy, what was she doing talking to her in the middle of a cooking instruction? "May I talk to her, princess?" he asked, reaching for the phone.

Lucy shook her head and listened carefully to what was being said on the other end. Then she said, "Okay" and "Bye, Ellie," and finally handed Pete the phone. "We need corns arch, Daddy," she said as she slipped her small pink thumb into her mouth for comfort.

Pete ruffled her curls, then put the receiver to his ear. "Hi," he said to Ellie, and his heartbeat quickened instantly at the sound of her voice.

"Lucy is a sweetie," Ellie said.

"Yeah. And itchy."

"Cornstarch compresses, Webster. Make a paste with lukewarm water, fold it into a cloth, and let her hold it to her face. If you don't have cornstarch, use baking soda. And also—" She paused, and Pete could hear noise in the background and someone asking a question. Then she came back on the phone.

"You're in the middle of class," he said.

"Yes. And you're going to fall way behind, Webster, but maybe I'll give you an assignment to work on at home."

"Homework . . . hmm. What if I need a tutor?"

Her light laughter filled him up inside. "I need to go, Pete, but be sure you don't give Lucy aspirin. It's not good for kids when they're sick like this. What am I saying? I'm sure you know that. Oh, and if you can stop by tomorrow, I'll send some yogurt Jell-O home for her. It will taste good if any pocks show up in her mouth or throat."

For a while Pete stood there holding a dead phone. But inside he felt very alive.

Instead of waiting until after work, Pete showed up at Ellie's back door at noon the next day.

"Pete!" she said. "What are you doing here?"

"Yogurt Jell-O lured me."

She laughed. "It's only noon."

"Would you believe I was in the neighborhood?"

She motioned from where she was sitting at the island to come in. "Corny line, Webster." She felt an inordinate joy seeing him there in his fancy suit. The feeling leapt up inside of her, then somersaulted once or twice. When it finally settled down into a gentle river of pleasure, there was a flush on her face and a brightness in her eyes.

"It's true," Pete said. "I was supposed to meet with this guy in Old Town about some work for his bookstores. An emergency came up before I arrived, so here I am, with time to spare." He walked his fingers along her arm. "And I thought to myself, what better way to spend it than in Ellie's kitchen?" He pulled out the stool next to hers and sat down.

She laughed and wrapped her legs around her stool. "And how did you know I'd be home?"

"A hunch."

"How's Lucy?"

"Still itchy. But my sister came over and Lucy loves playing with Rachel, so she'll be okay."

"The Jell-O is right there," Ellie said, pointing to a plastic container filled with colorful, wiggly figures. The yogurt Jell-O turned out to be strawberry- and orange- and lemon-flavored molds shaped like cats and teddy bears and giraffes.

"She'll go nuts over these, Ellie. Thank you."

"Good. There's enough for P.J. too. And one for you."

"Which one?" He glanced at the array.

"The cub."

Pete noticed a small bear with a baseball cap on his head. He laughed. "How do you know so much about kids?"

"I was one once." She looked down at her arm where his fingers were now rubbing gently back and forth. An expensive massage would have been no match. She looked back up to his face. "My mother used to do things like this for us when we were little. She also made great Mickey Mouse pancakes. We loved it. And now I make these little gizmos for my nieces and nephews when they're sick, and they love them too."

"They're pretty crazy about *you* as well."

"It's mutual. Having them is the best of all possible worlds. I can spend time with them, then come home and live my own life, without worrying about all the things parents worry about. It's the ideal way to blend children and career."

Pete listened, but he couldn't quite keep it all in focus. She was so tuned in to kids, something Elaine had never been. And Ellie obviously loved kids. She'd be a fantastic mother. He didn't say the thought out loud, because he knew instinctively it wouldn't be well received.

"Do you want something to eat?" she asked.

"Nope."

"What then?"

He shifted on the stool so that his knees opened, and he slid her own stool between them. "You."

"Me?"

"Yep." His fingers played with loose strands of hair at the nape of her neck.

Ellie was so keenly aware of the pressure of his thighs on hers, she could barely speak. "With or without mayo?" she asked in a fruitless attempt at levity.

He nuzzled her neck. "It's not you, Ellie, it's this incredible smell about you." His voice was a tantalizing whisper against the soft skin of her neck.

"Garlic?"

"And wildflowers and blueberry jam. All sorts of wonderful, sensual things."

She squirmed. "You don't make my life easy, Webster," she finally managed to say through lips gone dry and a heart racing. "You were much easier to handle when I didn't like you."

"Ah, so you like me. A start, Ellie, a definite start."

He nibbled lightly at her skin, and Ellie thought she would probably jump right out of it in ten seconds. "Pete, wait—"

He lifted his head but kept it close to hers, just inches away. His eyes were filled with desire, and she knew her own matched his.

"Ellie, I'm not asking you anything you can't handle, honest. But something is sure going on between us. And I think we need to give it a chance."

"Pete, it won't—"

"—work? I always thought that was such an inane line. What is *it*? And what does *work* mean, anyhow? We're talking about two adults who genuinely *like* each other. And in addition to that, there's this marvelous, miraculous chemistry going on that does something to *both* of us every time we get within shouting distance of each other. My life has been full to the brim with business and raising kids for a while now, and this is new to me, El. But I'd like to see what it all means, let it play itself out a little. What do you think?"

She looked at him with such raw need that he gathered her in his arms, nearly tipping over her stool. He kissed her gently, then held her apart once again. "I know your life is hectic right now. I've got a lot on my plate too. But what I'm proposing is this. At the least, I'd like to bury the baggage of that disastrous blind date and start fresh."

"Sounds possible," Ellie said.

"And maybe we could admit to some basic things, like the fact that seeing each other adds a whole lot to a day, that there are things about the other we'd like to explore."

She wet her lips, then nodded. "I think that sounds okay."

"And then—"

She shook her head. "Now I'm getting nervous, Pete. I'm not sure we need to talk about 'and then's.' The now is about all I can handle these days, and sometimes I don't do a terrific job of *it*."

"That's fine, El. My life doesn't lend itself much to elaborate plans either."

The phone rang, but Ellie didn't move to get it, and Pete ignored it. After her message played, a man gave his name and number and asked whether Ellie could give a cooking demonstration to his army reserve unit.

Ellie's and Pete's laughter merged together and wove a wonderful web around them. Inside it Ellie felt content and happy. The problem was, she thought, one didn't walk far inside a web.

The next several days flew by. Ellie was busier than she had ever been in her life. More articles appeared in local magazines, and she'd even been approached by a national periodical about an article featuring the new trend of men in the kitchen. She was successfully winding up her first course to rave reviews from the

men, their girlfriends, wives, and even strangers who
called to say they had been to dinner parties serving
"her meals" and how could one get the recipe for
moules marinière, or her leek and pecan pheasant?

Somehow, in the middle of the hubbub, she and
Pete managed daily contact, at least a phone call if
they couldn't actually see each other. They were both
wary in this dance they were performing, and whenever things reached a feverish pitch, they pulled apart,
each one fearing what kind of "and then" would be
attached to consummating the whirlwind of emotion
that had gripped them.

It was midnight one night when Pete finally got
to the telephone.

"I missed you," he said without preamble.

Ellie's laughter was throaty and coated with the
pleasure his call brought her. "I was on my way to
bed."

"Somehow I'm sorry you mentioned that."

Ellie slipped beneath the top sheet, cradling the
phone beneath her chin. Her loose hair cascaded over
her shoulders. She smiled into the cool shadows of
the small bedroom. She had been sitting there on
the edge of her wide oak bed thinking about him,
reluctant to go to sleep without talking to him. Then
he had called.

"Are you in bed?" she asked.

"No, I wouldn't dare call you from there. I'm
in my den, sitting in a worn leather chair that was
the only thing Elaine allowed me to keep when she
redecorated our old place. The TV's off, the window's

open, a cool breeze is billowing the curtains, and I can see the sky from here."

Ellie looked out her second-floor window. Through the tangle of tree branches was the sky, holding up a half-moon. "I see it too," she said.

"Nice."

She nodded as if he could see her, as if they were somehow side by side beneath that blanket of blackness.

"Ellie," Pete said, his voice suddenly serious, "I have a meeting in California this weekend. A short trip. Would you come with me?" He hadn't intended to ask her that. In fact, he hadn't really thought about it, only about how much he would miss her while he was gone.

Ellie's eyes opened wide.

"We won't be gone long, and I need to see you away from egg yolks and spatulas."

"Away . . ." she said, as if he had spoken a foreign language, one she was struggling to understand.

"Just for two days. I have an extra ticket."

"I have a million things to do here, Pete. Things are really skyrocketing with the business. I've got new courses to plan, interviews—"

"You need a break, El."

That was true enough. Franny and Harve had insisted she take some time to smell the roses, as they put it. Harve offered to take her fishing in Wisconsin, Franny suggested shopping.

"Well, I'm not crazy about fishing or shopping . . ."

"What?"

"Nothing. I'm thinking, that's all. Where in California?"

"Wherever you say." He was breathing faster now.

"I thought you had a meeting?"

"I do. In Monterey. One hour, max. Then we can go anywhere you want. It'd only be two days."

"It's probably a terrible idea—" Ellie waited. Pete was silent on his end, not refuting it. If he had, if he had tried to argue it, she probably would have made a different decision. He hadn't argued, though. He had allowed the dangerous element to hang out there, untouched.

Two days, she thought. Two days, alone with Pete. "Somewhere quiet . . ." She assumed she was thinking until her own hushed voice reached her ears.

"Absolutely quiet."

"With the ocean."

"Lots of ocean. All the ocean you want."

"What about the kids?"

"Taken care of."

"Just the two of us."

"There're a few people who live there, but we can avoid them if you want."

"I've never been to California."

"That settles it, then."

And somehow it did.

Plans fell into place as if some higher force were at work. Fran was thrilled and claimed it would give her some time to put the files in order so Ellie could make some business decisions when she returned. She'd take all messages, she said, and Sara would water the plants.

So that's all that was required, Ellie thought, to take care of her life in her absence: someone to take messages and someone to water the plants. The unusual thought made her sad, until she convinced herself it must be nerves. Nothing in her except emotion was urging her to go on this trip, and that was enough to unnerve even the calmest of souls. Every rational thought she managed to muster screamed, *Stay home, for heaven's sake! You have a business that is about to take off! Don't let yourself be sidetracked!*

The voices were dimmed by her heartbeat, though, and she agreed to let Pete pick her up at seven A.M. Saturday morning, provided he return her to that very same doorstep the next evening. And in between, well, in between she'd forget about everything in the world and allow herself thirty-six hours of . . . of . . . of relaxation.

Ellie nearly choked on the thought as they sped toward O'Hare Airport, but she didn't say a word. Pa always said, once you make a decision, make the most of it. Don't dilute it with backward glances.

Her first impression of California was of color—crisp, piercing blues and brilliant greens, yellow-gold and vermilion—and of a flowery scent.

"So this is California," she said as she settled back in the rented convertible.

"Oh, you haven't seen anything yet, Ellie. This is the tip of the iceberg."

As they drove through the Santa Cruz mountains on their way toward the ocean, Ellie believed him.

The winding highway was lined with Monterey pines and thick-trunked redwoods climbing up the hills all the way to the brilliant blue sky. A short while later the hills fell back, and the road Pete picked to take them down to Monterey wound through resort towns with names like Santa Cruz and Capitola and Aptos. Pete pointed to a small sign beside the road as they drove past a rolling field of spikey artichoke plants. Gilroy, it read, pointing to the east.

"Garlic capital of the world," he said above the rush of the wind.

Ellie held her head back to catch the breeze and laughed with delight. "A cook's paradise."

"Next time we'll wander on over," Pete promised. "But this trip isn't for Ellie the cook. This trip is for Ellie the person." He looked over at her and saw the tentative smile on her face. A lot of things had gone unspoken between them; there hadn't been time to discuss specifics about the trip. Pete was determined above all else not to frighten Ellie. He would be sensitive to whatever parameters she set. It would take Herculean strength—he wanted Ellie more than he had ever imagined wanting a woman—but he hadn't brought her to California to seduce her. He had brought her to be with her, away from the entanglements that constituted their separate lives, to know her apart from all that. And that's what he'd do.

While Pete met with his clients in Monterey, Ellie wandered around the history-rich Cannery Row on the Pacific shore. She could nearly smell the sardines that once had been packed in the old brick factories, filled now with colorful boutiques and eateries. By the time the hour was up and Pete wandered down to the spot where they had agreed to meet, her arms were loaded with packages.

He relieved her of a few. "What is all this stuff?"

"Gifts."

"For whom?"

"Everyone. Whenever my pop traveled, he always brought each of us a souvenir. The tradition stuck, and now everyone does it."

"But there're so many of you—"

"And that's why I have so many packages. Oh, and that green sack is for P.J. and Lucy."

"My kids?"

"The only P.J. and Lucy I know. I figured since I have their dad for the weekend, the least I can do is take a little something back as a thank-you."

Pete opened the sack and peered in at the boomerang with the Monterey Bay Aquarium decal on its smooth surface, and the delicate black-haired Indian doll, complete with a beaded necklace. "El, this is real nice. I don't know how you knew, but they're perfect gifts."

"Good."

"Maybe you can give them to them yourself."

Ellie wouldn't commit to that, and instead of answering, she changed the subject, informing Pete that she was starving. Her interior clock said it was well past her lunchtime.

They wandered arm in arm across the street to a casual restaurant on the water that offered a spectacular view. Sitting at a tiny table, they watched sea lions in the distance clapping their flat, slippery flippers and barking hoarsely. Sailboats drifted by, their brilliant sails puffed up gloriously, and they feasted on soft-shell crab, washing it down with crisp white wine.

"I didn't know heaven was in Monterey," Ellie murmured.

"Stick with me, baby," Pete growled in her ear, "and we'll make it all the way to paradise."

She shivered and swallowed a long drink of wine. "Where do we go from here?"

The waitress brought their check, and Pete slipped her his credit card. "From here," he said to Ellie, "we go to my favorite spot on earth. It's an hour south as the road meanders."

Comfortable silence filled the stretches between light talk as the bright yellow convertible serpentined its way south, past Carmel and on to the mountains of Big Sur.

"I've never seen anything like this before, Pete," Ellie said as they crossed Bixby Bridge. Pete slowed the car, and they looked out over the mountains on one side and the ocean on the other, suspended hundreds of feet up above an exhilarating gulf of air.

"They say it's not for the faint of heart," Pete said.

"Well, I was never that," Ellie said, laughing, and she reached over and rested her hand on his thigh.

"No," he murmured. "I would have guessed not."

Still, she did feel slightly dizzy as she looked out over the chasm separating her from anything solid, and her fingers tightened on Pete's leg.

"You do forget real life in a place like this," she said as they drove along Highway 1. The giant redwoods and pine trees that lined the road crowded in on them. In places, the road darkened as the towering ancient trees nearly blocked out the sunlight. Then they fell back and the road breathed again.

"The place we're headed," Pete said, "is just ahead. It was built a few years ago by a relative of one of Big Sur's earliest settlers."

Ellie could see nothing but trees and land and sky as they turned off the highway, drove through a gate, then followed a narrow, winding road that headed west toward the ocean. As they reached the top of a hill, she looked down and saw roofs of small cabins poking through the trees with the ocean beyond.

Pete parked in front of a small elegant reception house, where they were offered champagne in front of a fireplace while their reservations were processed. After their luggage was transferred to a van, a tan, blond man drove them up and down a hill to where they would stay. To the right of the narrow road were modern cabins built right up in the trees, accessed by black spiral staircases. The structures were all redwood and glass and angles. "We call them tree houses," the young man said. "But you're on the cliff side. These two right here."

The van stopped and Ellie and Pete got out. At first she didn't know where to look, then she spotted

slanting roofs that seemed to grow directly out of
the ground, covered with thick grass and ablaze with
wildflowers. Beside the house, a walkway wound down
to a wide wooden door.

"It's like a place we visited near my grandparents
in Kansas," Ellie said. "The early settlers built sod
huts like this."

Pete just smiled, then stood back while she walked
through the open door. A short distance inside, Ellie
stood stock-still. "Oh, Lord," she said. The cliff-side
cabin, filled with tasteful furniture, was a breath-
taking contemporary suite of wood and glass facing
the ocean.

"What do you think?" Pete asked as he fished
some money from his pocket for the driver.

She half-smiled, then said softly, "I don't think I'm
in Kansas anymore."

He laughed, feeling instant pleasure in the delight
that filled her words.

While Pete listened to the young man's directions for the elaborate sound system, the refrigerator,
bar, and supply of bottled waters, liquors, snacks, and
gourmet coffees, Ellie wandered around the beautiful-
ly designed cabin.

A bank of windows along the whole west side
of the suite looked out over the ocean. The walls
and ceiling were wood, slats of warm earth tones.
On the wide wooden bed, built out from one wall,
were fat Indian-print pillows and a down comforter
covered in blue denim. Facing the fireplace was a deep
couch with a half-dozen colorful pillows softening the

hand-carved back. On the other side of the fireplace was a bathroom as big as Ellie's bedroom. It, too, had windows with a drop-dead view of the sea, and placed strategically in front of them was an enormous whirlpool tub lined with slate.

"Do you like it?" Pete whispered into her ear.

She half-turned, her eyes still taking in the art pieces on the wall and the black bedside lamps that looked like Giacometti sculptures. "I shared a room with two sisters growing up," she said slowly. "The only hotels we ever stayed in were Holiday Inns, where kids went free. And as an adult, I've never taken a vacation other than going up north with my brothers or sisters or friends to stay in a tiny cabin half this size with six of us vying for the bed. Oh, and visiting my grandparents in Kansas."

"Then that's a yes, I guess."

She laughed softly.

"Come here," he said, and walked her over to the windows. It wasn't until they stepped outside onto the small patio that she realized the dwelling was built into the side of a cliff. The patio was a narrow level space that looked out over the sea before the cliff dropped off. Hundreds of feet below, the ocean thundered and seafoam rose high as the waves crashed against the jagged rock.

"Almost makes you forget cooking schools, doesn't it?" Pete said.

"And advertising campaigns?"

"Absolutely. Gone." He wrapped his arm around her shoulders, and for that moment, the world of business and kids and daily decisions fell away and the most important thing to do was breathe deeply enough to smell the sea and the wildflowers waving on the steep slope beside the cabin.

"How did you find this place?" Ellie asked.

"I found Big Sur years ago when I was at Stanford. My college friends and I came down and camped on weekends and breaks. And before I was married, I came a lot. Then later on, I'd come by myself. Elaine hated the ruggedness of it; she thought it was lonely here. So until the kids were born, I'd steal a weekend whenever I could. Sometimes I'd bring a backpack and sleeping bag, nothing else, and camp out under the stars. It doesn't matter how you do Big Sur, elegantly like this or with nothing. It just matters that you're here."

Ellie imagined Pete sleeping out under the stars, his long body wrapped in a sleeping bag. Had there ever been a woman with him?

"I've only been to this resort once before," he went on, connecting with her thoughts. "I was here shortly after it opened, and I stayed in this very room. I vowed then that I'd be back, but only when I could bring someone to share it."

She smiled. The breeze was cool, but inside she was as warm as toast.

"And now, fair lady," he said, "how about I give you a few minutes to get settled while I take my things next door."

"Next door?"

He cupped her chin and looked down into her

eyes. "This trip isn't about pressure, darlin'. It's about getting to know each other. I'll be within a bird's call from you, right under the next roof of wildflowers. And we'll take things easy. Be back shortly . . ."

He left before she could say anything, and Ellie stayed there on the patio, staring out at the sea. The waves below, she thought vaguely, were no match for the swelling of her own heart and the surging of desire that pounded inside her. How had this remarkable man tumbled into her life? And what was she going to do, now that he was there?

Pete returned in a short while and suggested they use the rest of the daylight hours hiking up into the Ventana Wilderness. Ellie agreed happily. She needed to get out of the cabin and away from that bed. She slipped a sweatshirt on and announced herself ready.

Pete had changed from the slacks and shirt he'd worn for his meeting to jeans and hiking boots and a bright blue windbreaker. She looked him over and said, "You look good, Webster. Hiking suits you nicely."

Pete returned the perusal, his gaze running over the jeans that fit her the way jeans should and well-used boots that had been through many seasons of rough Chicago weather. Her hair was back in its braid, curved thick and golden between her shoulder blades and frizzing out around her temples and nape. She wore no makeup, just a touch of sunscreen that gave a shine to her lips and a blush to her cheeks, and he was convinced that the less she tried, the more beautiful she was.

"Okay," he said, his voice suddenly thick, "I pass, huh?"

"Unless I meet a really good-looking bear," Ellie said, and moved toward the door. Lord, could she be trusted in the woods with this man? She suspected that the slightest breeze, the smallest brush against his body, might send her into orbit. She felt on fire around him. "Forest fires," she said out loud. "Are they a problem here?"

"None that we can't handle," he said, and closed the door behind them.

They drove part of the way, then parked the car, found the trail head, and set off. They walked single file, Ellie in front, up a rugged pathway that wound its way through thick groves of redwood and oak trees.

"Do we know where we're going, Webster?" she asked.

"That's a loaded question, Ellie," Pete said. He had toyed with the same thought while alone in his room. Out here in the wilderness, with Ellie so close he could almost feel her heartbeat, he wasn't at all sure he knew where they were going. It had *felt* right to bring her here where they could spend time away from everything else. What he hadn't counted on was the effect being with her in this wild, pristine place would have on the ever-deepening feelings he harbored for her. Or maybe those feelings had been there for a while now, and the power of nature was setting them free in some unexplainable way.

"What did you say, Pete?" Ellie asked, glancing back over her shoulder. "You're mumbling."

Instead of answering, he edged closer and tickled her neck with his fingertips.

"Careful, Webster. For all you know, you've latched on to a wild person here, and the slightest wrong move could unleash the savage beast inside me."

"You are sort of savage," he said, touching her hip as they climbed over thick tree roots that formed steps in the forest. "I'll have to be careful."

They hiked in easy silence for a ways, through forests and meadows and along narrow, flower-lined trails. In some places the trees, towering above them with branches stretching out like so many arms, blocked out the sunlight. The air grew cool and dark, the smells of the decayed underbrush more pungent. Pete pointed foliage out to her along the way, plants with perfect names like monkey flower and Indian paint-brush. They stopped and rubbed their fingers along the surface of oyster mushrooms thriving on the side of a mossy tree.

And Ellie, breathing in the otherworldliness of it, fell completely beneath the spell of the land.

Finally they reached the peak Pete had been aiming for, a perch so high, Ellie thought she could see eternity.

He sat on the scrubby earth, pulling her down between his legs. He wrapped his arms around her. "What do you think?"

"I don't want to ruin any of this by thinking." From where they sat, she could see the ocean in the distance, thousands of feet below, and between their

perch and the water were striped ridges of the Santa
Lucia mountains, in browns and deep greens and tans.
It was eerily silent, with only the hushed sound of
wind and an occasional flapping of wings, as birds,
curious about the intruders, flew over them.

"This makes me feel as though we're the only
people in the world," Pete said. He lifted her braid
and rested it over one of her shoulders, then rubbed
the nape of her neck.

"It could fool you, couldn't it?" She rested back
against him, her head touching his chest in easy famil-
iarity. All the tension of the past weeks began to drain
from her body. "My brother Danny would love this.
He's our family camper."

"The closeness in your family is nice," Pete said.
"You're lucky."

"You and your sister are close."

"Sure. But it's the interweaving of your family that
gets to me. All of you caring about each other, keeping
traditions. That's what I want to build for my kids."

"Then you will, Pete."

"I don't have much to fall back on, but we kind of
invent as we go."

"It has to start somewhere. We add traditions, too,
like bringing presents back from trips."

He played with a stray lock of her hair. "It would
be easier if I weren't a single parent."

"I don't think the number of parents makes the
difference. It's the depth of caring and attention and
love."

He nodded, his cheek rubbing against hers. She

Get Swept Away To Your Romantic Holiday!

Imagine being wrapped in the embrace of your lover's arms, watching glorious Hawaiian rainbows born only for you. Imagine strolling through the gothic haunts of romantic London. Imagine being drenched in the sun-soaked beauty of the Caribbean. If you crave such journeys then enter now to...

WIN YOUR ROMANTIC RENDEZVOUS PLUS $5,000 CASH!
Or Take $25,000 CASH!

Seize the moment and enter to win one of these exotic 14-day rendezvous for two, plus $5,000.00 CASH! To enter affix the destination ticket of your choice to the Official Entry Form and drop it in the mail. It costs you absolutely nothing to enter—not even postage! So take a chance on romance and enter today!

Has More In Store For You With 4 FREE BOOKS and a FREE GIFT!

We've got four FREE Loveswept Romances and a FREE Lighted Makeup Case ready to send you!

Place the FREE GIFTS ticket on your Entry Form, and your first shipment of Loveswept Romances is yours absolutely FREE—*and that means no shipping and handling.*

Plus, about once a month, you'll get four *new* books hot off the presses, *before they're in the bookstores.* You'll always have 15 days to decide whether to keep any shipment, for our low regular price, currently just $11.95.* **You are never obligated to keep any shipment**, and you may cancel at any time by writing "cancel" across our invoice and returning the shipment to us, at our expense. There's **no risk** and **no obligation** to buy, *ever.*

It's a pretty seductive offer, we've made even more attractive with the **Lighted Makeup Case—yours absolutely FREE!** It has an elegant tortoise-shell finish, an assortment of brushes for eye shadow, blush and lip color. And with the lighted makeup mirror *you* can make sure he'll always see the passion in your eyes!

BOTH GIFTS ARE ABSOLUTELY FREE AND ARE YOURS TO KEEP FOREVER, no matter what you decide about future shipments! So come on! You risk nothing at all—and you stand to gain a world of sizzling romance, exciting prizes...and FREE GIFTS!

*(plus shipping & handling, and sales tax in NY and Canada)

ENTER NOW TO WIN A ROMANTIC RENDEZVOUS FOR TWO

Plus $5,000 CASH!

or take $25,000 Cash!

No risk and no obligation to buy, anything, *ever!*

Winners Classic

SWEEPSTAKES
OFFICIAL ENTRY FORM

☐ **YES!** Enter me in the sweepstakes! I've affixed the destination ticket for the Romantic Rendezvous of my choice to this Entry Form. I've also affixed the FREE GIFTS ticket. So please, send me my 4 FREE BOOKS and FREE Lighted Makeup Case.

Affix Destination Ticket of Your Choice Here	TICKET	Affix FREE GIFTS Ticket Here	🎁

PLEASE PRINT CLEARLY   CK123   12237

NAME _____

ADDRESS _____

CITY _____ APT. # _____

STATE _____ ZIP _____

There is no purchase necessary to enter the sweepstakes. To enter without taking advantage of the risk-free offer, return the entry form with only the romantic rendezvous ticket affixed. To be eligible, sweepstakes entries must be received by the deadline found in the accompanying rules at the back of the book. There is no obligation to buy when you send for your free books and free lighted makeup case. You may preview each new shipment for 15 days free. If you decide against it, simply return the shipment within 15 days and owe nothing. If you keep them, pay our low regular price, currently just $2.99 each book —a savings of $.50 per book off the cover price (plus shipping & handling, and sales tax in NY and Canada.)

Prices subject to change. Orders subject to approval. See complete sweepstakes rules at the back of the book.

Don't miss your chance to win a romantic rendezvous for two and get 4 FREE BOOKS and a FREE Lighted Makeup Case!

You risk nothing—so enter now!

could feel his body warmth spreading directly into her. "You're right. But I want the most for them, you know?"

She heard the intensity in his voice, the depth of his caring for the two children around whom he was building his life. "You'll do it, Pete, you will. They're lucky kids."

He brushed the hair from her cheek and dropped a kiss in its place. "Well, all I know is at this very moment, I feel like the luckiest man on earth."

Ellie snuggled back into his embrace. She felt it, too, an incredible sense of well-being that had little, maybe nothing, to do with the real world. "It's these mountains that do it, and the ocean, the smell . . . They all weave a spell."

A shadow above them drew their attention, and they looked up, shading their eyes against the late afternoon sun. A black-shouldered kite hovered silently over them, treading air with its narrow, falconlike wings. Its bottom side was dazzlingly white.

"He's looking at us," Ellie whispered.

"Mythology says he's here to capture a soul and take it into flight."

The bird moved on, flying off into the setting sun.

"I guess he saw that ours were already occupied," Ellie murmured. She turned her head so she could look into Pete's eyes.

"It's going to be dark soon," he said, his eyes locking onto hers. "It hurts me to say it, but we need to head back."

"No. Not yet. Not before you kiss me, Pete." She turned farther and wrapped an arm around his neck. "Right here, on top of the world."

"I think I can manage that," he said, and he kissed her with all of his desire for this woman who had brought such unexpected joy into his life.

When they returned from the ridge and walked into Ellie's cabin, the sun had sunk completely into the ocean, leaving the sky in ever-darkening burnished streaks of color. They sat in one of the Adirondack chairs on the narrow patio, Ellie nestled comfortably in Pete's lap, and watched the drama play out before them, the night creep up into the sky. Behind them tiny lights above the cabin door went on, casting shadows across their still figures.

Pete breathed in the miraculous smell of her and pulled her closer, his hand sliding over her abdomen, his lips touching her ear.

Ellie sighed and closed her eyes, opening herself to the spiraling sensations.

"You cold?" Pete asked, tightening his hold.

"Cold? How could I be cold?"

The desire in her voice hung heavy on the night air. Pete felt it deep down inside himself. Instantly, as if shot by an arrow, he hardened with passion.

"You better be careful, El," he said in a tight, thick voice.

His words were a tickling breath along her neck and she stirred, her hips moving instinctively.

"I think when you're in Big Sur, Pete," she said softly, "you do what nature tells you to do."

"Is that so?"

"That's what I think, anyway." His hand was beneath her shirt now, running hot trails of fire across her midriff.

He kissed her neck while his fingers slid upward along her cool skin. When he touched her breast, his hand cupping the firm globe, she shuddered.

Suddenly she leaned forward in his lap.

"Ellie?" he said, his voice touched with surprise.

She didn't answer. Instead she slipped her sweatshirt over her head. In the next moment she undid the buttons on her shirt and peeled it off, dropping it in a puddle on the stone patio floor. In one single movement, her bra followed.

When she turned back toward him, her face bathed in the soft glow of the patio lights, her eyes were glistening with tears.

NINE

"I haven't felt this way for a long time," Ellie whispered. She smiled in the pale light.

It was the most beautiful smile Pete had ever seen. He sat still, his breathing shallow and uneven. "Oh, Lord, Ellie," he said, his words part prayer, part wonderment. She was even more beautiful than in his dreams, a perfect Aphrodite, formed by the gods.

With his hands at her shoulders, he held her slightly apart, drinking her in with his eyes. Then his hands slid down her arms, and his lips found the tender hollow of her throat. He kissed her there, then trailed his mouth over the smooth silken skin of her shoulders and down to the swelling sides of her breasts. He nuzzled the cleavage between them, rasped his tongue across first one nipple and then the other.

Ellie's head dropped back and her eyes closed. Incredible sensations swept through her, one after another, the pleasure so strong, it bordered on pain. An earthquake, she thought vaguely. She was in

California and she was experiencing her own private earthquake.

A cold wind whipped up from the ocean, ruffling the pile of clothing at their feet.

Ellie shuddered and Pete rubbed her arms. "Goose bumps," he whispered, and rose from the chair, lifting her in his arms. "We can't have that." As if she were weightless, he carried her into the house.

Two small lights illuminated his way to the wide bed, where he laid her gently among the fat pillows.

She looked up into his eyes and smiled.

"Now what?" he said, his gaze roaming across her beautiful breasts.

She ran a finger down his chest. "I don't know if I ever told you this, Pete, but sometimes—well, once, anyway—I walked in my sleep."

"That can be a dangerous habit."

She rolled her head toward the windows. "Especially with that cliff out there."

"Then I don't think you should be alone tonight, darlin'."

"Would you mind?" she asked. Her voice was husky, sensual.

Pete swallowed around the lump in his throat. "Ellie," he said, suddenly serious, "are you sure?"

She reached up higher and rested her palm on his cheek. "Everything inside me—my mind, my soul—wants to love you, Pete. Here. Tonight. I don't think there is more certainty than that in life."

"Without regrets?"

"I promise I'll still respect you in the morning."

She could feel the buildup of tears again, and she hoped Pete would understand what it was all about. Emotion, pure emotion. "I want you, Pete. And it feels right and good. That's all I know."

Pete bent his head to kiss her again. His desire was so strong, he felt heady, dizzy.

Ellie tugged lightly on his belt buckle. "Not fair, Pete."

His slow smile sent shivers of anticipation through her. As she watched, as still as her heartbeat allowed, he shrugged out of his jacket, peeled off his shirt and pants, and slid down beside her on the bed.

"I want to look at you," she whispered, lifting herself on one elbow. "I want to see every single, wonderful bit of you." She trailed a finger across his chest, through the thick patch of dark hair. Teasing a strand of hair, she saw that the slightest touch on his skin caused a reaction in other parts of his body. They were so completely tuned to each other, she felt that not only her body, but her soul as well, was bared to him. Instead of frightening her, the feeling excited and pleased her.

"You're a witch, Ellie," he murmured.

"But a good one, Pete. You'll see."

He leaned forward and settled her back against the plump pillows lining the head of the bed. With sure movements, he loosened the fastening on her jeans, then slid them down her legs and tossed them off the end of the bed. When he bent down to remove the rest of her clothing, she stroked his back and arms. She felt the muscles tighten beneath her fingers as he hurried. She wanted to touch every inch of him, to run her hands along his chest, his back, his legs.

Lying back beside her, Pete tipped his long body towards hers until they were pressed length to length, hips touching, hearts beating rapidly. His hands wandered over her lovingly, stroking her thighs and drawing delicious patterns of fire across her flushed skin.

Abandoning herself to the rush of heat in her body, Ellie rolled over onto her stomach, her small hand sliding over his naked body.

Pete moaned, the pleasure so sharp and unexpected that he could barely breathe. It flashed up his loins and across his chest. "Oh, Ellie," he gasped. "You're making me crazy."

"Hmmm" was all she answered as her fingers stroked fire on his body.

"You may be cooking up something you can't handle, my love."

"I never cook up things I can't handle, Webster," she said. Her laughter was low, filled with desire.

"Come here, my darlin' chef." Pete wrapped his arms around her and pulled her to him. She came easily, her body firm against his, breast against chest, thigh against thigh. He closed his eyes, breathed in the delicious fragrance that was Ellie, and nuzzled her ear. Without needing to see, he dropped dozens of kisses along the column of her neck, and he prayed that this incredible fantasy would not go away if he did open his eyes.

It didn't. When he opened them a minute later, Ellie was as real as his breathing, more lovely than in his dreams. "Sometimes, darlin'," he said, slipping a lock of hair behind her ear, "I can't believe this is all real. You . . . me—"

She ran a finger down the side of his face and around the curve of his ear. "For this moment, Pete Webster, for right now, it's the only thing that is real in the world," she said, then drew his mouth to hers, kissing him with a fierceness fed by her desire. Her tongue curled about his. Their kiss began and ended and began again, without a pause for breath, until Ellie was dizzy with the rising passion within her.

"Slowly, my darlin'," Pete whispered in her ear. "I want to give you the moon and the sun and the stars. . . ."

"I can almost touch them," she said, her words labored.

"I've dreamed of this, Ellie, of you and me."

"Pete . . ." Her eyes misted again, and she blinked back the tears. "Pete, I want you . . . I want you to love me. . . ."

He slid over her warm, flushed body. His warm gaze held hers, adoring her, wanting her. "Yes?" he whispered.

"Yes! Oh, Pete, my darling Pete—" She wrapped her arms around him, holding tight.

She was so beautiful. Slender and muscled, sleek, like a goddess who had slipped through the night and down into his bed. He bridged his hard, strong body over her.

"My sweet Ellie," he murmured, and unable to wait another moment, he slid inside her, filling her with all his pent-up passion and desire and need.

Ellie felt Pete surge within her, felt her whole body reach out to him, welcome him, and lift with him toward the sun and the moon and the stars, until all she could see and feel was the bright, blinding explosion of her life in his, his in hers.

When she could think again, breathe again, she held Pete tight, her hands curved around his buttocks, wanting that one moment to last for the rest of her life.

He rolled over and she lay quietly in his arms. As his breathing slowed and caressed her face, she thought about this man who had slipped into her life. This man whose touch, whose smile, had come to mean so much to her. This man she knew she was beginning to love.

A small fear leapt into her heart. What had they done here in this unreal place? What had they begun?

Pete stirred then, opened his eyes, and looked at her with such tenderness, her fears dissolved like so much mountain fog beneath a bright noon sun. She slipped closer, nuzzling his neck, pressing her body into his until they were one.

And then they slept.

Pete got up at dawn and pulled on his jeans, then walked silently out to the patio. He couldn't stay there beside Ellie without touching her, without loving her again. They had both awakened several times during the night, reached for each other in half-sleep, and begun it all again, the loving and discovery that seemed to be new with each touch, each kiss.

She looked so blissful now, a small lovely smile touching her lips, her face still and beautiful, that he would let her sleep. For a while. For as long as he could stand it.

The early morning air was cool, and a light fog hung over the water far below. The surreal feeling it created seemed to fit the whole weekend. He had gone to Ellie's at noontime those weeks before, when he had found her in her kitchen, to get her out of his system. Instead he had pulled her directly into his heart. He loved her, he knew that now.

Their night of loving had been so much more than a union of bodies, a few hours of sex. He wasn't sure he even understood it himself, but loving Ellie as he had, had released feelings that must have been harbored for a while now, feelings he had denied, pushed aside beneath work and the kids and daily routine. Now they were flung out there in the light of day, feelings that had a life of their own, and he didn't have the faintest idea what to do about them.

He shoved his hands into the pockets of his jeans and looked out over the water, peering through the haze, but there were no answers there. Maybe there weren't any answers anywhere.

Once you have heaven, he wondered, how do you handle earth? How do you keep it from imposing itself on you again? He wanted to hole up with Ellie in their special sod house for the rest of his life.

"Hi," said a sleepy voice behind him.

He turned and looked at Ellie standing in the open door. She was wrapped in a thick terry robe with the resort name on its pocket, her slender body nearly invisible in its folds. Her face was flushed with sleep, her hair tangled about her cheeks and neck. She took his breath away. "Hi, yourself," he managed.

She walked on out and wrapped her arms around his waist. "Do you know we missed dinner last night?"

"It crossed my mind once or twice."

"And?"

"And I figured we had our own five-star meal going."

She rubbed her cheek against his bare shoulder. "You did what you promised."

"Which one?"

"You promised me paradise, Pete."

He nodded. "Takes two to paradise."

"We were pretty good at it, if I do say so myself."

Pete was silent. "Good" wasn't the word he'd use. They had been magnificent together. Perfect. No, even those words didn't do justice to the emotion he had felt. Having Ellie beside him now completed it all. But going back to Chicago hovered over them like a hawk, and he wanted it to go away, to hover somewhere else.

"You're thinking of Chicago and real life," she said. "Don't, Pete. At least not for another few hours. Until we have to board the plane, let's just be. Just you and me and this wonderful place that you've brought me to. Certainly a few hours of uncomplicated bliss can't hurt, can it?"

She had tumbled directly into his thoughts, but it didn't really surprise him. There was some kind of direct link between them; he had felt it for some time. It was something he had never had with Elaine. He had never known what she was thinking or even why. And although privacy was a big thing with him, having Ellie connected so intimately to him brought him deep, satisfying pleasure. He felt the familiar pressure inside him, felt himself harden and his breathing grow shallow.

Ellie felt it too. It seemed almost inevitable now, that what he felt, she felt and vice versa. She looked up at him and smiled. "Did you see that big bathtub in there?" She inclined her head toward the sunken tub.

"I did."

"I'd like to soak for a while. Watch the sun lighten the sky. But it seems a shame to fill that giant tub for one person."

"A shame, huh?"

"And a waste."

He looped his arm around her. "Definitely a waste. They take their water very seriously here in California."

"So . . ." She ran a finger down his chest.

"So I say let's play the ecology game. Let's preserve a little water when we can."

And they did.

Ellie walked onto the airplane three hours later with great reluctance. Her life that day was different from her life the day before. Maybe it hadn't happened in that one day, embraced by the magic of Big Sur. Maybe it had been a seed that she hadn't felt growing until suddenly there was fruit. However it had happened, it was real, existing there between Pete and her. Something real, something alive, and with a life of its own.

Pete shoved their small suitcases into the overhead rack and sat down beside her, reaching for her hand and swallowing it in his own.

"It's as if we're afraid to let go," she murmured, looking at their fingers woven together.

He nodded.

"I haven't thought about cooking classes for almost two days."

"Does that bother you?"

"It surprises me. It has consumed me for weeks now, kind of like a newborn baby, I guess. Getting away from it is nice, but getting back to it will be nice too." She paused for a minute, then went on. "I'll be busy when we get back, Pete. Your course ends in a couple of weeks, and soon I'll begin two new ones. And I have several interviews this week, and some decisions to make."

"Our Ellie is going to be a star," he said.

His voice was lazy, but there was something in his words that made her look over and explore his face for hidden meanings. "I'm going to be a success," she said carefully.

"That's very important to you, isn't it?"

"Yes. But we still have four blissful hours in this airplane together before we're thrown back into that busy life. So let's not talk about what's ahead, Pete."

He must have heard the desperation in her voice, for he lifted her fingers to his lips and carefully, while she absorbed every delicious sensation, he kissed each fingertip with a tenderness that seeped all the way into her heart.

The next week was filled with stolen hours and telephone conversations filled with longing. When Ellie confessed to Pete that she had to sit on the kitchen floor beneath the wall phone because the cord wasn't long enough, he sent her by special delivery a fold-up cellular phone that she could take anywhere.

"Pete," she said, calling him on the new phone immediately. "You can't send me stuff like this."

"Why?"

"It's expensive."

"It keeps you close to me, Ellie m'love. Try and put a price tag on that."

She couldn't, of course, because he was keeping him close to her as well, and that was worth all the gold in Fort Knox.

The rush of attention she was receiving from the media was a blessing, she decided. It kept her from thinking too deeply about her personal life and allowed her, instead, to bask in the joyous feeling of it all for now. When things quieted down, she promised herself, there would be time to think.

"This week will be the last class for us," Pete reminded her the next Monday night when he stopped by her house on his way home from work.

"It's hard to believe that," she said. "It went by so quickly. On the other hand it started a lifetime ago."

She snuggled into the warmth of his arms. "This class will always be special to me."

He nuzzled her neck. "As well it should, my love. But don't get any ideas. You're not throwing this baby out with the bathwater."

She laughed, then slid her fingers into his hair and kissed him hungrily. "No," she murmured. "How could I ever throw this baby out?"

Ellie approached the last class with mixed emotions. She hated to see these men leave, to *graduate*, as they insisted on calling it. They had become friends as well as students. And in this class she had met, or remet, Pete. In this class, somewhere in between burning soufflés and roasting chickens, she had fallen in love. But she couldn't think about that tonight, she told herself. Tonight was for the men, their grand hurrah. And this thing with Pete, this wondrous, joyful *thing*, would have to be explored later.

Ellie had told the men this last class would be their final exam; they would each be given a recipe, the ingredients, and one hour to prepare it. Then they would all feast on the delicious results. The kitchen was ready, sparkling clean, the work stations were filled with fresh vegetables and pork tenderloins and new potatoes. Both Sara and Fran had come to help, and small certificates were signed and sealed in crisp, official-looking folders. Included with each was a bound copy of the recipes the men had mastered and special cooking tips on what to cook for what occasion: a weekend with the kids, the boardroom blues, impressing someone special, and so on.

"The end and the beginning," Fran said, her eyes lighting up with pride for her sister, her hands clasped over the beginning bulge that was her and Harvey's fifth child.

"You sure you're up to this tonight, Franny?" Ellie asked.

"I wouldn't miss it for the world. We're ready. Bring on the chefs."

They came just before eight, but with their own surprises. The men were dressed in handsome, elegant tuxedos with colorful satiny cummerbunds, a secret gesture they'd decided among themselves the week before. And they carried bright white chef's hats, as tall and as puffy, Tex said, as Ellie's best soufflé. Embroidered in small navy letters were the words *For Men Only.* The hats, Pete explained, would stay with her, to be used by future students.

They also brought gifts of flowers and wine and aprons, two new food processors, and enough glass baking dishes to more than replace those they'd broken as they'd learned to cook.

"What is all this?" Ellie said, her hands pressed to flushed cheeks.

"It's a special night," Pete said. His hands stayed at his sides, but his eyes told her he did so only with great effort.

"These are tokens of appreciation, Ellie," Tex added. "Everybody sort of had the idea at once. And it's our little investment, you might say, in the future of 'For Men Only.' "

"Inspired by my dropping the fork into your mixer a while back," said Jake. "It hasn't been the same since."

They all laughed, and another man added, "Don't think we didn't notice your great restraint, Ellie, when the wine supply was diminished by our friend Tex's tasting technique."

"Guzzling the whole bottle—is that the technique you mean?" said Harold, and they all joined in laughing and remembering the minor fiascoes that the course, and Ellie, had endured.

"Okay, enough foolishness," Ellie said at last. "If we don't get started here soon, you'll never get home tonight." Her eyes met Pete's, but she tore her gaze away. As much time as they managed to find for each other, it was never enough. Pete had a whole life apart from her, and she did as well. Those short days at Big Sur had been more blessed than either of them realized at the time, and there were nights when memories of them were Ellie's only consolation.

"Okay, gentlemen," she said, ignoring the catch in her throat. "Let's get started. Tonight you're on your own. The recipes are at your work stations, you'll work in twos or threes, and you should be able to do everything required in one hour. And then," she added with a grin, "we'll eat ourselves into oblivion."

They set to work, and in minutes the kitchen buzzed with activity. Sara and Fran circulated and helped fetch things, cleaned up spills, and joined in the cheery banter that accompanied the preparation of walnut-escarole salad, orange-flavored pork tenderloin, and an herbed acorn squash soup that was as colorful as it was fragrant. Sara, clearly smitten with Pete, stayed as close to him as possible. Ellie smiled as she overheard Pete gently teasing the teenager, then complimenting her on the things Sara worried about, like her natural curly hair. He must be a wonderful father, she thought. He said and did all the right things—and the thought filled her with a strange poignancy.

The men stuck to the schedule and in one hour, they were setting the table.

"When can Harvey get in one of these courses?" Fran asked, watching in amazement as knives and forks and spoons ended up in the correct places, salt and pepper shakers appeared, and a beautiful flower arrangement materialized in the center of the table.

Nothing was burned on this special night, and they all sat down to an incredible feast, complete with carefully selected wine, toasts, and the presentation of diplomas.

Just after the last diploma was presented and cups of espresso were passed around, the telephone call came.

Ellie, assuming it was Harvey calling to check on Fran, stood in the archway between the dining room and kitchen and grabbed the phone.

Talk continued around the table while she covered one ear and listened to the caller. When she hung up, she stood there for a minute, leaning against the archway, her eyes slightly glazed.

Pete was the first to notice. He shoved back his chair and moved to her side. "El, what's wrong? Are you okay?"

She looked up at him and nodded. The beginnings of a smile lifted the corners of her lips. "That was a friend of mine who works for one of the local television stations. Official word will come tomorrow, she said, but she wanted me to know ahead of time. Her station wants me to teach a class . . . on television . . ."

"That's terrific, Ellie!" Tex boomed.

Everyone else jumped in with congratulations and questions and toasts to Ellie the television star.

Ellie was in a daze. Way back when her cooking school was in the planning stages, she and Fran had toyed with various fanciful scenarios. A sort of "what if" game, and Fran had come up with a television cooking show. It was simply a dream, a fuzzy idea that she had forgotten about. But here it was, out in front of her. And it wasn't a dream at all.

All the men helped Sara, Fran, and Ellie clean up, and soon they were gone. Pete left, too, going home to relieve the sitter. He had left quickly, Ellie thought, as she lowered her tired body into a hot sudsy tub a short while later. She rested her head back against the rim of the tub and replayed the evening in her mind. Pete hadn't said much to her after the phone call came about the television show, she mused. When she had put away the linens, he had followed her. He had shut the door, holding it closed with his foot while he kissed her slowly and, she thought now, emotionally. But then someone had knocked on the door and they had pulled apart. There hadn't really been time to talk. Or maybe he hadn't wanted to.

A while later, relaxed and sleepy, Ellie pulled on a threadbare gown and slipped between the sheets of her bed, her mind playing with images of Pete. Wonderful Pete. He had probably stayed in the shadows that night on purpose.

The excitement of the whole evening swept down on her once more—the ending of her first successful course, the men's generosity, and the incredible news about the television show—and she found herself drifting off on a whole medley of emotions. She pulled her grandmother's quilt up to her chin and hugged thoughts of Pete around her as she did every night. Soon she was asleep, dreaming of television lights melting her chocolate soufflé and *People* magazine begging her to be on the cover. And the most handsome, wonderful man in the world standing quietly in the shadows.

TEN

The television show was going to be taped on a Friday and, Ellie told Pete, the producer wanted "real men." "I suppose that means we can't make quiche," she added.

Pete laughed. It was noon, and he and Ellie had met in a coffee shop on Michigan Avenue for lunch and as much touching and cuddling as they could get away with in the shadowy back booth.

"I feel like I'm in high school," he said with some annoyance.

"I'll take what I can get, bub," Ellie said in a sultry voice, her hand crawling into his lap.

"Hey, there, darlin', careful," he growled into her ear. "A *real* man can take just so much."

"Okay," she said demurely, folding her hands on the table and looking into his eyes.

"Now that you're behaving and I can breathe again, there's something I want to ask you, El."

"Hurry and ask, because I can't behave for long."

"I'd like you to come to dinner at my house with me and my kids."

"Oh, Pete." Her voice dropped, her insides constricted. "I don't know." She had talked to Lucy and P.J. several times on the phone, including the night they had called to thank her for the presents from California. Even over the phone, she had felt her heart reach out to them. But the truth was, she didn't want that kind of attachment. It was unfair to the kids, she told herself. And to her. Seeing her and their dad together, the kids might create false expectations. "I'm not sure it's a very good idea right now," she said carefully.

"I don't understand, El. You love kids."

"Yes, but children sometimes get the wrong idea, and that's not fair to them. I've seen divorced friends muck that situation up royally. Attachments are so easy to form, and until you know what's going to happen—"

"Ellie, all I'm asking you to do is come for dinner. I'm not asking you to move in." He covered her hand with his own and his tone lightened. "I want to impress the kids with my newly learned barbecue techniques. I might need some help."

The waitress interrupted to fill their water glasses and flirt with Pete, giving Ellie a little time. When the waitress left, she deftly changed the subject.

"So what do you think about this 'real men' idea?" she asked.

Pete frowned, confused for a minute, then pulled together the threads of the earlier discussion. "Oh, the producer—"

"Actually the producer is a woman. But she wants to have men on the show with me. She wants me to teach a class to men, not cameras."

"Probably a good idea."

"But scary, don't you think? This new course I'm teaching, for example. I taught a class on baking the other night, and the recipe called for cream of tartar. The CEO of Northland Manufacturing, a very bright fifty-year-old man, used tartar sauce in his cookie mix."

Pete laughed. "You didn't appreciate what gems you had in your inaugural class."

"Oh, indeed I did." Her hand slipped back down on his thigh.

Pete took a long swallow of ice water.

"Pete, I want you to be one of my real men. You're the realest man I know." She smiled before continuing. "And I'll ask Tex, Jake, and maybe Harry."

"They'll be great, but not me, El. I was your worst student."

"Not true, Pete. Well, maybe sort of true, but you ended up completely adequate."

"Thanks a lot."

"I mean in the *kitchen*, Pete. You're spectacular in most other areas, and one man shouldn't be the best at everything."

He slipped an arm around her and rubbed his thumb on her neck. "Ellie darlin', I don't want to be on your show, but I appreciate the invitation."

"Pete, please. I want you there."

He took the check from the waitress and pulled out his wallet. Inside him, conflicting emotions tumbled about. Ellie's business was beginning to impose itself on both of them. It was this other *thing* out there, this presence that demanded so much of her. He was happy for her and frustrated over it at the same time. The best way to handle it, he had decided, was to remove himself from it. Out of sight, out of mind.

"Please, Pete," she said again.

He wavered. Then an idea hit him. He considered it for a few seconds, then said aloud, "How about this, El. How about we make a deal here."

"A deal, huh?" she said suspiciously.

"An eye-for-an-eye kind of deal. A trade, so to speak."

She leaned her head to one side and looked at him, eyebrows drawn together.

"A television appearance," he said slowly, "for a barbecue."

She was silent. He ran his fingers along her neck. "It's time they met you, El. It's not a big deal. They've met friends of mine before."

Ellie pushed a smile in place. He had her. She suspected they were both resisting each other's ideas for reasons that had nothing to do with the actual situation. If he could give in, she supposed she had no choice. "Okay, Pete. That will be fine." She smiled coyly and added, "In fact, it's probably a good idea. Maybe I should make house calls on all my students to check on how they're doing in the kitchen. Kind of a post-op checkup. Imagine—all those bachelor pads." Her brows rose suggestively.

"Not on my life," Pete said, and dropped a kiss on her nose.

She wrinkled her nose. "I love it when you do that," she said, then slid out of the booth. Turning back toward him, she leaned over and kissed him full on the mouth.

"Hmmm," he said, his arms reaching for her.

"Just dessert," she said, and pressed her palm against his cheek as if to absorb the feel of him so she could take it with her. "And now I'm off in a rush to meet Mary Elliot, my *producer*." She drew the word out dramatically. "And I'm going to tell her she's in luck because the most terrific bachelor in Chicago has generously committed himself to our show. And if she dares get close to him, I shall make duck soup out of her."

"Producer soup," Pete corrected as she left. His whole body filled with pleasure from her presence and her touch, and the lovely look of her as she wound her way across the coffee shop and out into the crisp autumn sunshine.

On Friday Pete showed up at the television studio just a few minutes before taping time.

Ellie had been worried that he wouldn't show, and she scowled at him from across the room. She couldn't hold it, though, and as Mary Elliot ushered him across the cable-ridden floor to his place on the set, her scowl dissolved into a lusty look sent behind Mary's back.

Pete smiled, savoring it, then turned his attention to Mary Elliot and the bevy of orders she was peppering him and the two other men. By the time the lights were turned on and the cameras were wheeled into place, he had nearly forgotten that he had almost reneged on the show at the last minute.

He sat on the tall stool assigned him and placed one foot on the rung, looking up at Ellie. She was on the other side of a wide island, checking over the food and bowls and wooden spoons. Her hair was in its usual cooking-class braid, a thick golden plait down her back, and she wore the familiar white blouse, crisp white apron, and blue jeans. But there was far more to look at than clothing and hairstyle. There was Ellie's incredible beauty, her unique loveliness that still took his breath away. And that, he thought with a barely suppressed wave of desire, she wore the best of all.

Ellie herself was such a bundle of nerves, she could hardly think straight. She and Mary had decided on a relaxed format, no cue cards, just Ellie doing her thing. Whatever *that* was, Ellie thought, looking at the platter of chicken breasts lined up in front of her. Could she pull this off? And would men actually watch *For Men Only*? Or would they all be tuned in to CNN and ESPN? It was far too late to worry about things like that, however. Besides, it was only a taping. If things went haywire, they'd simply take their scissors or whatever they used and snip the snafus out. She took a deep breath and smiled a wobbly smile at Mary, who was standing in the shadows. Then she looked at the three men on the other side of the island, shrugged a small shrug, and said in a pleading whisper, "Guys, I need you."

They all smiled encouragingly, then a man behind them counted backward and the room grew quiet. Ellie smiled and wet her lips. They were on.

She focused on her erstwhile students, the men she had gotten to know so well, and she relaxed as soon as she started talking to them. "You guys probably believed for a long time that if you worked hard and were successful, there'd be someone there to cook for you." She paused, smiled, and said with gusto, "Not necessarily true."

With that, she took off, her stage fright evaporating in the heat of the lamps as she did what she did best.

The men forgot about the cameras too. They were one hundred per cent with Ellie, watching her swing knives around with more finesse than Rambo and pound chicken breasts to thin slivers with a few well-aimed blows.

They produced, too, following her familiar directives, laughing and joking as they competed with one another for the most imaginative sauce and the lightest turnovers. When Tex sneezed, Ellie threw him a towel and a "Bless you," and informed the audience always to sneeze into sleeves and napkins, never into the food. When Jake's slippery chicken breast landed on the studio floor, Ellie, much to the chagrin of the scurrying cameraman, picked it up, turned on the tap water, and explained to the audience that all a fallen chicken breast needed was a little scrub down, which she proceeded to demonstrate. "Waste not, want not," she said to the camera with a wise smile, then returned the breast to a smiling Jake, along with the suggestion that he use a heavy dose of fresh tarragon on it.

When Tex's sautéed meat stuck to his pan and resisted a neat removal with the spatula, she reached across the counter and speared it with a fork. "Don't let your food get the best of you, Tex," she admonished, wagging a finger. "Always let it know who's boss."

She peppered her instructions with conversation, telling the men about her friend who left her lover eleven times because of his disposition and returned eleven times because of his chicken soup. And she talked about the quality of cooking that appealed to her the most: its certainty. "When you turn up the heat," she said, "water boils. When you put butter and flour and liquid together over heat, it thickens. Always, without fail. So much more dependable than the Dow Jones average."

When Mary gave her the three-minute signal, she was ready for it. Instructing the men to hold their dishes up for the folks at home to see, Ellie closed her eyes and breathed in the delicious fragrance, so that her face revealed the ecstatic sensations that the television viewers were missing. Then she told the men it was time to pour the wine and toast their success, to kick off their shoes and to enjoy.

As for the television audience, she turned and

thanked them for coming, told them that they, too, had the potential to turn butter and eggs and herbs and ordinary chicken breasts into culinary masterpieces. With a wave of her oven mitt, she wished all her new friends a good day and a light soufflé. On either side of her, Pete and Jake and Tex lifted their wineglasses in a cheery adieu.

There was a second of silence during which Ellie stood frozen to the spot. Then movement and excited voices reached her ears, and she breathed again. In the next moment Mary was at her side, wrapping her arms around her. "Ellie," she said, "you were wonderful."

"Wonderful?" Ellie repeated with some amazement. She truly didn't know what the end result of her half hour had been. For the entire taping she had been suspended above time and place. It was almost as if someone else had done the show. She caught Pete's eye and silently sought his opinion.

"You are remarkable," he said simply, looking at her across the tangled wires and intruding cameramen.

"But . . . ?" she said, sensing an incomplete thought.

"No buts. You're the best there is, Ellie." He walked around a camera and the island and took her into his arms, kissing her gently. "I mean it. And now I have to run. I've got a meeting in an hour."

Ellie watched him walk away and felt the cool air rush in between them. No matter what he said, somewhere in that space an ominous hesitation dangled from his words. Did he think she wasn't cut out for this kind of thing? Or was it more complicated than that? For a second the heady rush of a successful cooking program was replaced by a thin slice of fear.

There wasn't time to think about it, though. Mary took her by the arm to meet some station people, and she was forced to push the troubling emotions away. She could only deal with one thing at a time, and today it would have to be the show. Those other, more muddled feelings would have to wait.

Pete's barbecue was set for the next night, and Ellie thought about it all day long. Her feelings were as mixed as a bouillabaisse, and for once in her life she seemed totally incapable of working through it all.

Mid-afternoon Fran stopped by with Kevin and Georgie, her youngest boys, and she listened to Ellie try to sort through her feelings. As she removed a container of brownies from the cupboard, she said authoritatively, "You're in love, Ellie, that's all. There isn't always logic to it. Don't think so much."

"I didn't say anything about love, Fran," Ellie said as Georgie and Kevin dug into the brownies.

"It's in your eyes, sis," Fran said gently. "And your smile, your walk, the way you talk to me about him."

"I don't know what to do." Ellie stood before the sink and looked out over the small, square backyard. Leaves were falling from her one maple tree, covering the grass with a fall coat of vibrant color.

"Sometimes you don't *do* anything, El, you just—"

"Pete needs all sorts of things in a woman right now, Franny," Ellie interrupted.

"You seem to be satisfying him."

Ellie nibbled on her bottom lip, then she allowed a slow smile to soften her face. "He's wonderful, you know? He looks at me, really looks *into* me, and it's not my nose or lips or the color of my hair or the size of my waist and breasts he's looking for. He looks, and he keeps on looking until he sees all the way into my soul."

"And this is a problem?" Fran wet a dishcloth and began swabbing her sons' chocolate-smeared faces.

"He has these two kids—"

"You love kids."

Sure, she loved kids. That was a given. And she already liked little Lucy just from talking to her on the phone. But that wasn't the issue. She shook her head. "My thinking is muddled, Franny. Maybe you're right, maybe I'm worrying about something that isn't even worriable."

"I *do* know what you're saying, sis. What you want right now is to be an entrepreneur, a business success. You're on your way to that, and you don't want complications. You don't want to be a mother, not for a while. But as far as I can tell, no one is asking you to be one. So relax. I do think you're trying to buy trouble."

Ellie turned from the window and smiled at her sister. "Franny," she said, "what would I do without you?" She hugged her, then busied herself wrapping the rest of the brownies in foil. She handed them to Franny, gave Kevin and Georgie hugs, and waved them all off.

For a long while after they left, she stood at the

kitchen window. In the end she cemented her resolve to take her life moment by moment, to heed Franny's words for now, and to leave trouble alone until it came knocking.

Ellie drove to Pete's house in her battered Chevy and prayed it would make it from the city to the northern suburb. When she checked the address, then looked up a second time at Pete's home, she wasn't at all sure she was glad it *had* made it. The fifteen-year-old car was as out of place on the oak-lined street as a limo would have been on hers.

Evergreen Lane was a shaded haven of elegant family homes. Tall oaks and elms rose high into the sky, their branches bending over the street and casting dappled shadows on the wide green lawns. The homes were spacious and carefully kept, their leaves raked and gardens tended. But one-seventeen, the home at the address Pete had given her, was the loveliest of them all. It looked, Ellie thought, like something straight out of a movie set: the perfect family home. The home in which no one could possibly be unhappy.

She turned her little car off the street and onto the brick-paved circular drive. Stopping in front of the house, she turned off the engine, then just sat. She needed a minute to collect herself, to let the surroundings sink in.

The house was a two-story white brick colonial with a screened-in porch on one side, a three-car garage on the other, and magnificent flower beds with spectacular late bloomers still flowering everywhere. The grass that fanned out from the house was a soft green that made her want to lie down on it.

Inside the house, Pete had heard Ellie drive in. Her car had announced its arrival with a cacophony of coughs and sputters. He stood at the hall window and watched her sitting in her car, taking in the grounds, the house, the trees and flower beds. He wondered what she was thinking, if she was regretting her decision to come, the new connection she was allowing to be made. He had been cavalier about his invitation, but deep down he knew she hadn't bought it. He wasn't sure he believed it either. He *had* brought women friends to the house before, and he had involved them in things with the kids. But the difference was he liked those women as friends, and that was absolutely all. The kids didn't think any more about such visitors than when they went to Rachel and Paul's and met people there, or when neighbors and friends of Pete's stopped by. Ellie was different. So very, very different. And Pete, always so sure of himself, was suddenly wary of what he was beginning.

Outside, Ellie finally stepped out of the car, took a deep breath, and patted the hood of the Chevrolet. "It's okay, kid," she whispered. "I know exactly how you feel." That wasn't entirely true. She wasn't at all sure of what she felt, except that walking through the front door of Pete's gorgeous home was a new chapter in their life, just as going to Big Sur had been.

He opened the door before she had a chance to knock. Stepping out onto the brick steps, he took her into his arms, holding her close. "Hi, Ellie," he whispered into her hair.

"I almost went back home," she said, breathing in the familiar smells of him. She didn't attempt to move, safe there in his embrace. "I thought I had the wrong address."

"Why?"

She pulled her head back to look up at him. "Because I know of only two little Websters, and your gorgeous home-sweet-home is big enough for a family of twenty-four."

He shrugged. "Be prepared, I always say."

She laughed, then stepped back to put some space between them. "Here," she said, "these are for you."

In one hand she carried a shopping bag. In the other, a bunch of bright yellow daisies. She handed him the bouquet.

He smelled it, then drew her close again and dropped kisses on the top of her head. "Flowers . . . That's twice now," he said, his voice suddenly thick. "Twice in a lifetime."

She touched the petal of a daisy with her fingertip. "And if you behave yourself, who knows?"

"You'd better come in," he said, drawing her into the cool entry hall. "The kids are eager to meet you."

From the front hallway, Ellie could see all the way through the house and out to the back where sunlight rippled on a free-form swimming pool. The pool was surrounded by rocks and flowers and flowering shrubs, a cool blue pond in the woods that was his backyard. Nearby she spotted tricycles and Big Wheels and a swing hanging from the branch of a gnarled oak tree. "It's so lovely," she said.

"But you haven't seen it yet. Come on." He took her elbow and led her through the library, into a cozy den filled with books and a beautiful old desk with stripes of wood inlaid in the leather top. There was a brass telescope on a stand, a worn leather chair, and an oversized couch. "My sanctuary," he said with a grin, then walked her down a short hallway and into a family room and a kitchen that took Ellie's breath away.

Plump couches surrounded an enormous fireplace, beautiful cotton rugs were scattered haphazardly on top of the polished plank floors, an old library table along one wall displayed dozens of family photos. Comfortable chairs with colorful pillows made cozy conversational groupings. The family room and kitchen flowed one into the other, and in the latter there was an eating alcove that jutted out into the backyard, a half-circle of windows that welcomed in the outdoors. The wide refrigerator and oven, the abundant bleached cabinets and up-to-date appliances, overwhelmed Ellie. She ran her hand along a smooth marble countertop and sighed. "This room is a cook's paradise, Webster. You have absolutely no excuse for not being the premier chef of the city."

"I guess that means you approve."

She noted the pride in his voice. "It's wonderful."

"The instant I saw this place I thought, 'This is a perfect house for kids to grow up in.' I bought it that very day."

"Elaine was very lucky."

He shook his head. "Elaine never saw this place. The kids and I moved here after Elaine left."

"After?" Ellie said in surprise. So much for stereotyping. She had almost started to like Elaine, simply because this house was so perfect for raising a family, so lovely and elegant, comfortable and warm, all at once. It would have been any mother's dream home. "Where did you live before this?"

"A Michigan Avenue penthouse. It was so high up that I used to call the doorman in the morning to see what the weather was down below."

"I don't imagine it was an easy place to raise Lucy and P.J."

"Nope. It was hard to fit a swing set on the terrace, and P.J. was always in trouble for racing his Big Wheel in the corridors. And then there was the issue of the Snuffleupagus . . ."

"Snuffleupagus? Him I know—the big hairy guy on *Sesame Street*."

"Actually our Snuf is a sheepdog, but you're right about the big and hairy."

"You had a sheepdog in a Michigan Avenue highrise?" She laughed.

"No, not really. That was part of the problem. The kids and I, well, P.J. and I—Lucy was a baby—wanted a dog. Elaine and the condo management didn't."

Just then a huge ball of mottled gray fur barreled into the room and raised two hairy paws onto Pete's chest. Pete looked around the dog to Ellie. "He must have heard his name. Ellie, meet Snuf. Snuf," he said, looking at the dog, "this is the woman I've been telling you about."

Ellie scratched the dog's head. "And exactly what kind of stuff did he burden you with, Snuf?"

Snuf barked in response, and that sound brought in another flying bundle, this one far smaller and with a head of burnished curls that flew in every direction. She stopped short when she saw Ellie, then looked from Ellie to Pete and back again.

"Lucy," Pete said, "this is my friend Ellie. And Ellie, this is my favorite daughter, Lucinda Elizabeth Webster."

There was hesitancy in Lucy's huge brown eyes, Ellie noted. The tiny girl looked her over carefully, her gaze wandering up until her head was held back at an angle.

Ellie slipped down to her knees and held out one hand. "Hi, Lucy," she said.

Finally the smile came, slow and cautious, but vibrant enough to light up the whole room.

"I love Lulu Happy Dreams," Lucy said.

"You do, huh. I don't think I know Lulu Happy Dreams."

"Sure you do. She's my Indian doll."

"The one you brought her from Big Sur," Pete explained.

Ellie smiled, her eyes still on Lucy. "I'm glad

you like her, Lucy. What a nice name you've giv-
en her."

Lucy nodded in agreement. "She's an Indian maid-
en," she said wisely. "Daddy told me stories about
her."

Ellie squeezed her fingers into fists. She wanted to
wrap Lucy up in her arms and carry her off. Instead
she pulled a book out of her sack and handed it to
Lucy. "I brought you this book, Lucy. It was one of
my favorites when I was your age."

Lucy took the book and looked at it carefully.

"It's about a wonderful snowfall and a huge
snowplow named Katy. Maybe sometime we can
read it together."

Lucy nodded, and her smile widened as she thanked
Ellie and hugged the book to her small chest.

"Your dad was showing me your house, Lucy,"
Ellie said. "May I see your room?"

Now Lucy beamed. She nodded enthusiastically.
"And I guess I'll have to show you P.J.'s too," she
said. She looked up at Pete, her head cocked to one
side, the timidness completely gone. "And you can
make us drinks." Her small chin stuck up in the air,
her eyebrows lifting. "Okay, Peter?"

Ellie bit back her smile and took the small hand
that was held out to her, then she followed the small
child-woman up a winding flight of carpeted stairs to
the floor above.

They found P.J. in his room on the floor, his eyes
glued to jumping figures on a television screen and
his fingers wrapped tightly around two controls. "P.J.

is playing a game," Lucy said, then walked over and stood between him and the TV.

"Move, Lucy!" the slender boy yelled. Then he spotted Ellie and dropped the controls. "Oh," he said, frowning.

"Hi, P.J." Ellie said, smiling into a face that must have been a dead ringer for his father's thirty years before. "I'm Ellie. Sorry for interrupting your game."

"S'okay," he mumbled. He looked from Ellie to the screen, then reluctantly back to her.

She handed him the bag holding the remaining gift, hoping it didn't look like a bribe. P.J. wasn't nearly as happy as Lucy to see her. "This is for you, P.J.," she said, and started back toward the hall. "Maybe we'll see you later?"

"Sure," he said with obvious relief at their departure. Before Ellie and Lucy were out of the room, Ellie heard the clanging sound of the video game's resumption. She wondered if he had even opened the bag.

By the time she and Lucy had toured each of the six bedrooms on the second floor, made a brief stop in the cavernous attic on the third, and carefully checked seven walk-in closets and two clothes chutes, they were fast friends.

They walked back into the family room hand in hand and found Pete waiting for them with a tray full of drinks, a basket of chips, and a bowl of dip. From the direction of the terrace, Ellie could smell coals heating up in the grill.

She sat down on the couch and made room for Lucy beside her. "Lucy is a wonderful hostess."

"Lucy's great," Pete agreed, winking at his daughter as he handed them each a drink.

"And how about that chicken pox, Lucy?" Ellie asked. "Looks like the marks are all gone."

"They went to New Yorka," Lucy said.

"Majorca," Pete corrected.

"Uh-huh." Lucy's copper curls bounced up and down. "To my mother."

"You sent them to your mother?" Ellie asked.

"Yep." Lucy wiped some lemonade from her upper lip with the tip of her tongue.

"Elaine hadn't had the chicken pox," Pete said. "Her first photo shoot was fourteen days after the kids left her. Guess what the cameras found?"

"How awful!" Ellie ignored the look of divine retribution that flashed across Pete's face behind Lucy's back.

"The people couldn't take her pictures," Lucy said. "It made her mad."

"Sometimes things happen for the best," Pete said philosophically. "And now, ladies, it's time to get this show on the road. I don't know about the rest of you, but I'm starving."

Ellie followed him into the kitchen while Lucy disappeared to find her brother. "She's a sweetheart, Pete," she said when Lucy was out of earshot.

"And a pistol. You never know which face of Lucy you're going to get."

"And she has her father wrapped as tight as skin around her little finger."

He took the salad out of the refrigerator. "Maybe.

P.J. is a little more shy. He's a terrific kid, but not as sure as Lucy that he has the world by the tail. He had some rough days after Elaine left."

"He must have missed her. Lucy was too little."

"He thought it was his fault Elaine left."

"And now?"

"I think he's come around. But he's wise beyond his years and is going to make damn sure no one ever does it to him again."

"That's a tough burden for a boy his age."

Pete nodded, pouring Ellie a glass of wine. "True, but he could have worse scars, I guess."

"Does he relate well to his mother?"

"That's nearly irrelevant. He doesn't see her enough to relate to her. Once a year, tops. He didn't even get a birthday card from her this year."

Ellie's heart ached for the small boy upstairs.

"Fortunately, P.J. is close to me," Pete went on as he pulled food out of the refrigerator. "And that's definitely a plus. He'll usually tell me how he feels. I just don't want him souring on women at the age of seven. I want him to see that women can be pretty wonderful." He turned from the refrigerator and leaned over, nuzzling her neck. "Know what I mean?"

Ellie felt the tiny hairs on the nape of her neck lift to his touch. "Careful, Webster. The fire outside is probably enough for right now."

Reluctantly Pete pulled away. He looked at her for a minute before resuming his work, then said, "You make me so damn happy, Ellie. Have you any idea?"

She looked down, fiddled with her glass, then met his eyes again. Her own were drowning in emotion. "Yeah, Webster, I know. It's like a boomerang, you know?"

Pete nodded, coughed away the emotion that stole his breath for a moment, then busied himself with the food on the counter. He pulled the last items he needed from the refrigerator, arranged them all on the island, then picked up his wineglass. Clinking it to Ellie's, he said, "Well, what do you think?"

He had laid out the perfect weekend-with-the-kids meal, as Ellie had labeled it in her course: hamburgers, bratwurst, kaiser rolls, baked beans, and potato salad. Fresh crisp vegetables and a spicy sauce stood off to the side. The dessert was her foolproof, impossible-to-ruin cookies-and-ice-cream pie.

"You sure know how to impress a teacher," she said, snagging a carrot stick and dunking it into the dip.

"I sure try." He turned her hand his way and took a bite of the carrot.

"You sure do," she murmured.

The rhythmic beat of tennis shoes on hardwood floors stopped him from trying to impress her further. He stepped away and smiled as Lucy, followed by P.J., entered the room. In his hands P.J. held the ant farm Ellie had brought, and at his side, a loyal guard, was Snuf.

"What's that, sport?" Pete asked.

"She brought it," he said, nodding in Ellie's direction.

"She has a name. It's Ellie. Did you thank her?"

P.J. looked at Ellie, the frown still creasing his forehead. A sprinkling of freckles darkened his nose. He caught his lower lip between his teeth, released it, then gave a small nod. "Thanks."

"You're welcome," Ellie said. She smiled, then helped Lucy climb up onto a stool to reach the chips.

P.J. stood back, still holding the plastic container in his hands. Finally he looked up at Ellie. "How does it work?"

Ellie walked over to him. She had the odd sensation that if she walked too fast, he'd turn and run like a frightened deer. He didn't, and she looked at the box he had dropped on the floor. "I'm not exactly sure myself, P.J. I never had one of these, but my nephew Casey—he's about your age—says they're cool. Maybe we can figure it out together."

"My dad can do it."

"Not now, P.J.," Pete said. "I have to get these burgers on the grill."

"Can't she do that?" he asked, his eyes averting Ellie.

"This is my show. I'm cooking, not Ellie."

Ignoring the conversation, Ellie picked up the box and read the instructions, then, as if Pete and P.J. hadn't spoken, she took a sack of sand from the box and handed it to P.J. "I think somehow this has to go in this." She pointed to the plastic box.

While Pete watched, admiring her patience, she helped P.J. figure out how to pour the sand into the flat container. When she accompanied his son outdoors to find and capture a colony of ants willing to relocate, Pete's admiration grew by leaps and bounds. He knew it was curiosity over the ant farm that motivated P.J., rather than the beautiful woman helping him, but it was something. If he'd learned anything these past couple of years, it was to count small favors.

Later, while Pete and P.J. flipped burgers on the grill, Lucy and Ellie set the table in the glassed-in alcove. Lucy talked nonstop about dolls and preschool and her little friend next door. "Ellie?" she said as she picked up a fork from the floor and wiped it on her jeans.

"What is it, sweetie?"

"Do you like fires?"

"Well, I don't know, Lucy. What kind of fires?"

"Like the kind in my backyard." She pointed beyond Ellie, out the windows.

Ellie spun around. P.J. was standing calmly beside the stone grill, his gaze fastened on the leaping flames that were greedily devouring Pete's carefully prepared meal. Thick gray smoke rose into the air.

Ellie dropped the napkins. She was around the table in an instant and flew out the kitchen door with Snuf and Lucy in hot pursuit. Before she could reach P.J., Pete came out of the pool house and ran across the lawn.

"What the hell!" He pulled P.J. away from the grill and looked at Ellie. "What happened?"

Ellie scooped up Lucy. "I don't know. Lucy spotted the fire, and we got out here when you did." Her eyes lit on P.J. Next to him, on the ground, was an empty box of kitchen matches. She bit her lip and held her silence while Pete tried to salvage the dinner.

"It must have been the grease from the bratwurst dripping on the coals that caused it," he said. "I was only gone a minute to get some tongs from the supply cupboard in the pool house." He looked down at P.J. "You should have called me immediately, P.J."

His son shrugged.

"I don't think any of this meat is edible," Pete said, pouring baking soda on the flames.

"That's okay," Ellie said. "There's plenty of other food."

She felt P.J.'s gaze on her. She knew he had seen her looking at the matches. The box had been full when Pete walked out with it. P.J. must have dumped the whole box on the grill when Pete left for that one minute.

Pete sighed, then looked at Ellie and shrugged apologetically. "So much for my cooking expertise."

"Accidents happen," she said, and heard a rush of air leave P.J.'s lungs.

By the time they had put the fire out and brought things inside, the sky was darkening and P.J. was asking for pizza.

Pete, tired and short on patience, agreed and went into the kitchen to call in the order. Lucy followed to make sure they left off the pepperoni.

P.J. started after them, but Ellie touched his shoulder. "P.J.?" she said carefully.

He stopped.

"P.J.," she said in a low voice, "what you did was very dangerous. You could have hurt yourself."

"Are you going to tell my dad?" Snuf sat between them, looking sorrowfully from one to the other.

Ellie was silent. She saw the look in P.J.'s eyes, daring her and pleading with her at the same time. Finally she said, "This can be between us, P.J., but only if you promise me you'll never play with fire again."

P.J. nodded as Pete and Lucy returned. Then he moved to the other side of the room and assiduously avoided Ellie for the rest of the evening. Snuffleupagus, who had fallen in love with Ellie, divided his time between the two of them.

Ellie left soon after they finished eating the rubbery pizza.

She was nearly as tired as the kids seemed to be, and pushing the evening further would have been counterproductive. Even Pete seemed okay with her leaving, although the kiss he managed to squeeze in when he walked her to the car left them both feeling frustrated.

Pete called Ellie later that night, after the kids were tucked in and he had had a chance to stretch out in his soft leather chair with a double Scotch at his fingertips. An autumn moon hung low beyond the windows.

"So much for impressing the girlfriend," he said when she answered.

"That wasn't the impress-your-girlfriend menu, anyway."

"I forgot. That's the one served by candlelight on the veranda."

"Beneath a full moon."

"If I had tried that one, it would have rained."

"It's not your fault, Pete." Ellie was in bed, the light out, but wide awake. She was tired, yet the events of the past week—the television show, the new courses, and now tonight, this less-than-successful evening with Pete's family—were all churning around together, weighing on her, and pushing sleep beyond her reach.

"We forgot dessert," Pete said.

"I had plenty to eat."

"The damn pizza tasted like cardboard."

"Is food the issue here?"

Pete took a long swallow of his drink. He welcomed the burn as it ran down his throat and into his stomach. "My cut-to-the-chase Ellie," he said softly. "Just one of the many things I love about you."

"You know me, Webster."

"I'd like to be knowing you in all sorts of ways right now."

"There'll be other nights."

He sighed. "Sometimes it all gets to me."

"You do fine, Pete."

"P.J. isn't always so—"

"P.J. is fine, but you can't push him, Pete."

"I know. He's still working through some things. Lucy, on the other hand, thinks you're great. 'More pretty than Ariel,' to quote the expert."

"Now, that's a compliment."

"You know Ariel?"

"Of course. Some of my nieces and nephews gave me my own *Little Mermaid* video for Christmas."

Pete laughed.

Ellie leaned back into the plump pillows. Her body was beginning to relax. It was the sound of Pete's voice, its soothing timbre, stroking her across the miles. "Hmmm, this is nice," she said.

"Just you, me . . . and Ma Bell."

She laughed.

"It's frustrating, is what it is. You're miles away in a bed by yourself, and I'm here in a chair big enough to hold us both."

Ellie smiled into the dark. A sharp wind had picked up over the lake, and drafts of chilling air creaked through her old house. The sheets had been icy cold when she slipped between them. The extra blanket she'd taken from the linen closet helped, but she knew the only sure source of heat was Pete. "I wish you were here," she said softly.

"Me too."

"We can pretend."

Pete took another swallow of his drink. "I think my imagination has short-circuited tonight, El."

"Never. Give it that Webster try."

He kicked off his shoes, turned off the light beside the chair. "Help me."

"Okay," she said, her voice dropping to a dreamy, coaxing level.

Pete caught the tone and held it in his head. He started to free his mind to think only of Ellie, Ellie at the end of the line. Ellie in bed, the phone cradled by her shoulder and the pillow. He wondered what she looked like right now. Would she be stretched out, or curled into a question mark beneath her white cotton sheets? And her hair—that incredible hair— it would be slightly mussed, fanning out around her head like a halo. It was cold tonight; she probably wore a long nightgown, the kind that would slide up her smooth, beautiful legs with a gentle push of his hands.

"Webster," she said, her voice a purr now, "you're too quiet. Are you up to no good?"

"I'm up to your thighs," he murmured.

"I—I guess I won't ask about that." Ellie closed her eyes, smiling. Along her thighs she felt streaks of heat. She dug her fingers into her hair. "Are you in bed, Pete?"

"I'm in the den. Lights are out. Moon's hanging out there waiting to be touched."

"Me too. Waiting to be touched, I mean."

"I can almost feel you, El."

She burrowed beneath the blankets. Pete's presence was so real, she felt she could touch him, too, reach out her hands and rub them across his chest, twist her fingers in the rough, springy hairs.

They were both silent, playing with images of each other, thinking and feeling and loving across a sleepy city.

"Pete . . . ?"

"Hmm?"

"Are you falling asleep?"

"Don't know exactly, El. I feel I'm slightly above the earth, but I don't know if it's sleep."

"You seem so close."

"And you're right here, El, your head against my chest."

She turned her head. A warmth was rising up from her toes. "I guess we should go to sleep," she said. Her voice was groggy and she felt pleasantly tipsy.

"Maybe so."

The sound of his voice spun in slow motion around her, floated up to the ceiling of her room. A soft smile settled comfortably across her lips. Slowly, unnoticed, the bright blue telephone slipped down to the floor while undefined worries evaporated. In their place, dreams, wondrous and joyful, filled her head.

ELEVEN

Ellie hoped people would enjoy her televised cooking show when it aired the following week. She even imagined, when she allowed herself such flights of fancy, being asked to do another show, maybe around Thanksgiving or Christmas. A holiday show, helping men cook their way through special occasions.

But she had never, not in her wildest dreams, imagined the offer Mary Elliot and her boss laid out in the walnut-paneled conference room the week after the show aired.

"The phone has been ringing off the hook," Janice Jarvis, program director of the television station, said in her no-nonsense voice. "Men love it. Women too. It's a hit, Ms. Livingston. We'd like to do some more. An eight-week series and then we'll see what happens."

Ms. Jarvis paused to order coffee through an intercom, giving Ellie a moment to calm herself and to try to deal with what was being said. When Ms. Jarvis turned her attention back to her, she said, "I'm not sure I understand what you're saying." One of her knees began knocking against the underside of the table, making a rattling sound. She caught Janice Jarvis's irritated look and quickly pressed her hand against her leg, steadying it. Her heart was another matter.

"What we're saying is this," Janice went on, accepting the tray of coffee from an office worker. "We want *For Men Only* to be a weekly show. The shows would be taped, of course, and that could all be done in a few days. At the end of the eight-week airing period, we would look at our figures and decide where to go from there."

"I see," Ellie said. She wet her lips, forced a calmness into her voice, and said, "I'd want content control, of course."

Mary, the producer, spoke up. "Oh, you'd have complete creative control, Ellie. Absolutely. What I know about cooking would fit into a demitasse cup! I'd handle production and direction, but the cooking show itself, the menus, instruction, and all that, would be your domain."

"We'd like to draw up a contract for you and your lawyer to look at as soon as possible," Janice said.

Lawyer? Ellie immediately began rummaging through her mind for lawyer friends or relatives. She nodded, hoping her expression assured them her lawyer was waiting in the wings, always at her beck and call.

"I would want it clear in the contract," she said, "that ownership of any spin-offs—cookbooks, equipment, and so on—would be mine, licensed by my own company. And the money involved for the show itself would have to be sufficient to allow me to take this time away from my business. I will have to hire and train people to help me teach."

She paused and looked at both women. She couldn't believe she was talking to them like this. Could they read between the lines? Did they know that she would *pay* them to do this show? The publicity alone was worth thousands of dollars. She forced a smile to her quivering lips.

"I can see you're not a novice at this sort of thing," Janice Jarvis said.

Ellie delivered her best "of course not" smile.

"The offer," Janice went on, "will be generous, and, we think, indicative of the talent we feel you have for television. Of course, everything is negotiable."

"Of course," Ellie murmured into her coffee cup.

Four hours later, about the time Ellie was returning to earth in the homey warmth of her own kitchen, a courier showed up with the contract.

She scanned the pages of small print, her eyes searching for important items. She let out a whoop just as the phone rang, then calmed herself down to hear Fran's voice.

"Oh, Franny, you won't believe it," Ellie said, her voice rising with each word. "It's incredible, really. For eight television shows, they're offering me more than I have *ever*, in any of my dozens of jobs, made in an entire year. A *year*, Fran! I have to hang up now and scream."

And she did, in the shower, with the radio on in the bedroom so the neighbors wouldn't call the police. And then, still dripping, she called Pete.

Pete found himself smiling at her joy. He could feel it billowing along the phone lines as she talked. He forced himself to think of that, of her excitement and her pride and her happiness, and not where it was all leading. "Ellie," he said, "that's great. You deserve every bit of this. You are quite extraordinary, you know."

"No, I don't know that, Pete. But I do know that this will be a good thing for me. This is what I've wanted, what I've worked for. Someone to take me seriously, listen to my ideas. It's a wonderful feeling."

"So let's celebrate."

"I thought you'd never ask."

Pete planned it all, from the dinner at Spiaggia, where they sat side by side on an elegant rose-colored banquette and clinked their crystal wine glasses together, to the Four Seasons Hotel, where he carried her into a suite high above Michigan Avenue and set her on the magnificent king-size bed.

Ellie lay still, looking up at the ornate molding that surrounded the room. "This is so extravagant, Peter," she whispered. "We could have gone to my house, to—"

"Peter?" he said.

"In a suite as luxurious as this, you become Peter."
She smiled up at him.

He shrugged out of his suit coat and dropped it
on a chair. "Do I have to act like a Peter too?"

Crossing her arms behind her head, she watched
him moving in the shadows of the dimly lit room as
she pretended to give the question great attention. "I
guess it depends on the Peter. Peter the pope? Peter
the saint? Peter Pepper, or maybe Peter Ustinov?" She
giggled. Both of them had enjoyed the grand Italian
wines at Spiaggia and a wonderful amber-colored
brandy that had left Ellie feeling as loose and as
breezy as a kite. Nothing could touch her happiness
tonight.

Pete smiled at her whimsical talk, then stepped
out of his shiny black leather shoes. His French silk
tie was next, followed by his crisp white shirt. As
Ellie watched each movement, he continued his lazy
disrobing until he stood completely naked in the middle of the elegant room.

"Oh, yes," she murmured. "I think you've hit on
the perfect Peter behavior."

He walked toward her, handsome and self-assured
in his nakedness.

"Peter my knight," she said, as he reached the bed.

"In shining armor, Lady Eleanor?"

"The loveliest armor I've ever seen." Her gaze
was roaming over his beautiful body with the care and
attention allotted a great treasure. "Oh, Pete, you do
know how to plan a celebration."

"Nothing but the best for my lady love."

She reached out one finger and ran it down the long muscle of his thigh. "Would you care to recline with me, kind sir?"

Pete sat on the edge of the bed and looked down at her. Her silk blouse shimmered across her breasts, rising and falling seductively with each breath. "May I?" he asked, and unbuttoned a small hook at the neckline.

Ellie, a willing accomplice, pushed herself up against the headboard and let him slide the blouse over her head.

Next he slipped a finger beneath her bra strap and slowly pulled it off one shoulder, then did the same to the other strap. "Did I ever tell you that you have wonderful shoulders?" he asked, dropping kisses along the curve.

"I . . . I don't think it has come up . . . no."

"Well, it's true." He unsnapped the bra hook. Her breasts immediately fell free, two perfect globes lit by the soft bedside lamp. The lacy garment dangled from his fingers, then, as his eyes devoured the woman in front of him, it fell to the floor.

Ellie's lips parted in a sensual smile. She lifted her hand to his cheek and looked at him, his eyes, his mouth, then her gaze traveled down the full length of his body and back up again. "Thank you for bringing us here, Pete," she said, the words catching on the emotion in her voice.

He dipped his head and moved his mouth over her shoulder and down to her breasts, dropping kisses all along the way. "Oh, Ellie, my love," he said, his breathy words a butterfly wing against her heated skin, "we're not anywhere yet. You wait . . ." He continued the kisses, small ones at first, circling her breasts. Her head fell back and she closed her eyes. Ripples of desire rolled through her body.

Pete took one nipple carefully between his teeth and sucked on it gently until he felt her muscles loosen and her breath come in spurts.

"Oh, Pete—" she murmured.

"It's only the appetizer, my love. We'll go slowly, enjoy each course completely." With quick, easy movements he removed the rest of her clothing and deposited it on the nearby chair, then turned his complete attention back on her.

His hands roamed where his mouth had been, feeling, touching, exciting her with gentle, firm massages. He wanted this night to be perfect, a joyous, sensuous feast for the woman he loved. He dug his hands into her thick golden hair, then cupped her face and locked his eyes on hers. "Ellie, I do love you, so very much."

Ellie felt the crazy sting of tears behind her lids and blinked rapidly. "I love you, too, Pete."

And then, with the license love allowed, they boldly and generously gave to each other, caressing and holding and kissing, until Ellie felt the urgent hardness of Pete, his rapid breathing, the pounding of his heart. She looked into his eyes, her own glazed with the passion that had slowly and steadily built up inside her.

Without words, but with perfect communication, Pete pulled her over on him, holding her there, his hands firm on her buttocks.

"Sir Peter," she said, smiling down into his eyes.

"Lady Eleanor. I do believe it's time for the main course." He lifted her, ever so slightly, and brought her down fully on him, filling her completely. Her soft moan filled his head as her body tightened around him. He thrilled at her movements, at first slow and rhythmic, then increasing in abandonment until he couldn't stay still himself.

"My great love," he murmured, and a second later, with joined cries of great, heart-stopping delight, they exploded together in a wild, joyous leap of love.

They slept little, their bodies tangled together beneath the sheets, dozing, then waking and reaching for each other in a desperate kind of need. Ellie didn't want to think what it meant, this grasping for Pete's love. It was almost as if she were gathering it, bottling it all up, so it would still be within her if Pete himself disappeared. Those thoughts were disturbing, though, so she pushed them away and allowed herself this night of total joy.

In the morning they wrapped themselves in thick hotel robes and drank hot coffee at the tall window overlooking the city. Gusts of wind blew in from the lake, bending trees in the distant park and stripping them of their colorful coats. Pete and Ellie nibbled on croissants and touched each other in between bites, cuddling closer on the love seat.

"This must be it," Ellie mused. "This must be all that heaven allows. I can't imagine more."

"I guess we'll just have to see, won't we?" Pete said.

She nodded. There was a mixture of sadness and joy in the morning, and although she tried, she couldn't seem to pull the emotions apart.

"How is P.J. doing?" she asked. She had seen him several times since the barbecue, once when Pete brought the kids in to see the famous kitchen where he had learned to cook, and another time when he and Ellie took them to the circus. But most of their time together revolved around impromptu excursions, such as to an ice cream parlor or walking through a park. The outings were usually unplanned, Pete calling at the last minute or stopping by with the kids. At first Ellie protested, feeling somewhere inside of her that it wasn't a good idea, then she began looking forward to the trips, the visits, Lucy's small sticky hand tucked in her own. When she wasn't with them, she found herself thinking of them, of the slender boy with the protective shield wrapped tightly around him, and the little girl who was already attached to her heart. And P.J. liked her, too, Ellie knew that, even though he fought like crazy to hide it.

"P.J.'s okay," Pete said now. "A little leery of the world, as usual, but very into basketball. I'm coaching his team, and P.J. is really consumed by all that. Want to come to a game sometime?"

Ellie tried to imagine Pete coaching a whole gaggle of freckle-faced, uncoordinated little kids. The thought made her smile. "Sure. Sometime maybe," she said, but it was hard to make plans like that when she knew her own days were going to be frantic for a while.

"And speaking of invites," he said, "there's a payback we need to make for this night of bliss."

"There'd be no way to pay this back, Pete."

He lifted her fingers to his lips and kissed them. "Agreed. But there is something we need to do. My sister, Rachel, kept the kids last night, but attached a string. Dinner with her and Paul, her husband. She's in a tither because she hasn't met you. Thinks I've been keeping her from you for some dark, ulterior motive."

Ellie smiled. "Have you? Are you ashamed of me? Or maybe you're afraid she'll spill all your secrets."

His fingers crawled into her lap and slipped beneath her robe. "I've bared all to you, El."

She shivered. "You have, huh?"

"How about if I show you?"

Her whole body reacted to his touch, like a flower to sunlight. Pete led her across the room to the wide, mussed bed, where reality was tucked back into the shadows for one more blissful hour.

Pete did extract a promise from Ellie that they would both dine soon with Rachel and Paul, but Ellie's new working schedule warred against her social life. For two weeks straight she had to back away from promises to Pete in order to meet with lawyers and producers and to work on her courses.

"It's almost too much," she said to Fran one day

as they went over a brochure for the new courses. "Is that possible, that a dream can explode on you?"

"You'll have to set some priorities, but everyone has to do that. It's new for you because of Pete."

Ellie frowned. She didn't want to hear this now, but Fran went on.

"It's true, El. You only had yourself to think about before. You could work all day and all night if you wanted to. But there's Pete now."

"Pete has his responsibilities too. Lucy and P.J., to be specific."

Fran nodded. "That's right. There're two other people involved here. In the beginning, when you and Pete were getting to know each other, it didn't matter because it only involved the two of you. But it seems to me that things have become more serious, El. Maybe it's time you started thinking ahead. Where is it all going?"

"This from the very woman who shoved my fears beneath the rug."

"That was then. Things were different. It's clear to anyone who knows you that it's much more involved now. And that automatically brings in your *whole* life, and Pete's too. And that brings us to two little kids who don't have a mother to speak of, and not only that, but whose father *wants* them to have a mother."

"How do you know that?"

"Oh, Ellie, stop it. You know it as well as I do. Pete is the quintessential family man. That's all he wants for those kids—a genuine, old-fashioned, mother-father-dog-station-wagon family. He wants it desperately. I know that, not only from things you've said, but from Pete himself."

Ellie nibbled on her bottom lip. She couldn't deal with this, not right now, not with the business taking off like a rocketship and a dozen decisions to make. Not now . . .

"Now is the time, Ellie," Fran said abruptly. "Before someone gets hurt."

"Fran, I think you're jumping the gun on this. Pete and I haven't even discussed marriage."

"Not out loud. But Pete's thinking it, El. Trust me."

Ellie shuffled some papers, and when she met Fran's eyes again, her own were moist.

Fran reached across the table and squeezed her hand. "I don't mean to sound tough, Ellie. You've never loved like this before, and I think so many things are happening to you that it's hard to see them all."

Ellie was quiet for a minute, and when she looked back at Fran, a half-smile was in place, as well as the serious look of a woman with a lot of work to do. "Okay, Fran, but we need to get back to these brochures. They're overdue. That's what we need to deal with today." She shoved a stack of papers in front of her sister, forcing away the incomprehensible issue of the-rest-of-her-life.

Through Rachel's persistence, an evening was finally set when they could all meet for dinner. It had been three whole days since Ellie had seen Pete. Their separate schedules hadn't allowed a single free minute, and she raced out to his car when he pulled up.

"I've missed you," she said, sliding in beside him and wrapping her arms around him.

"*Missed* doesn't begin to describe it," he said, just before kissing her hungrily. And then, reluctantly, he moved from her arms and put the car in gear.

They drove in silence for a while, grateful simply to touch each other. "You look a little tired, El," Pete said when they had pulled off the expressway and onto the quieter, tree-lined suburban streets of Kennilworth.

"A little. It's a treat not to be cooking," she said. "It seems that's all I do these days."

Pete drove the Jag and Ellie's hair blew loose and free around her face and shoulders.

"That's exactly what I've been thinking," Pete said.

She pushed her hair back from her cheek and studied Pete's face. "It's been a busy time."

"Yes," he answered, his eyes on the road.

"Not Big Sur," she said softly. The words "Big Sur" had come to mean special things to them, the realization of their love, time away from time, the mystical, special togetherness that existed apart from the world.

"No, not Big Sur," he agreed.

For a few minutes there was no talk, just the strains of a classical piece on the radio. Then Pete said, "The kids ask about you."

Ellie was silent for a minute as a new feeling surged through her: guilt. She felt it rub against her chest, an uncomfortable, gnawing sensation. She looked over at Pete and said, not really knowing if it was true, "My life will calm down soon." Suddenly angry at herself for the hint of apology in her words, she talked about her business. "Did I tell you that a publisher is interested in my writing a cookbook for men?"

Pete nodded, forcing a smile on his face, and was almost relieved as he pulled into Rachel and Paul's drive. He didn't want to talk about her business, nor book offers, nor television shows. They were growing too big, a monster wedging its way between them.

Rachel was out on the steps before they lighted from the car, and she hugged Ellie as if she had known her for a lifetime. "I can't believe it's taken this long for us to meet," she said, then turned and introduced Ellie to Paul, her handsome, dark-haired husband. Another couple, neighborhood friends, stood just behind them.

Introductions were made all around, and the animated group, led by Rachel, made their way to the back of the elegant house, where they sat in a room filled with plants and lovely art pieces. It overlooked a garden terrace, ancient elm trees, and a lawn that rolled all the way back to Lake Michigan. In the large fireplace a fire burned merrily, sending dancing shadows on the paneled walls. Platters of appetizers—clams and stuffed mushrooms and tiny potato skins—filled the large square coffee table.

"I'm really impressed, Rachel," Pete said, coming up behind her. His gaze roamed over the tableful of delicacies.

Rachel laughed, a husky, uninhibited laugh that made Ellie decide that she and Rachel were destined to be friends.

"Everything looks great," Ellie agreed, smiling at the female version of Pete.

Rachel screwed up her lovely face. "It *should* look great," she said. "It's from my favorite cookbook." She tossed Ellie a small paperback.

As Ellie scanned the title, Pete read it aloud from over her shoulder: "*We Deliver: A Regional Guide to Restaurant Menus and Services.*"

"Notice the much-thumbed pages?" said Paul, and Rachel socked him playfully in the arm.

"Don't fret, my love," she said with mischief in her sparkling eyes. "I've solved all our culinary problems. I just happened to snag the last spot in Ellie's January 'For Men Only' cooking course." She winked sexily at Paul. "It's your Christmas present, babe. And I insist you pay special attention to the class on 'Amazing Aphrodisiacs.' "

Everyone laughed, and the tone of the evening was set. When Rachel got up to, as she said, "fool with things in the kitchen," Ellie trailed along to help. Rachel was without pretense and accepted greedily. "I need all the help I can get. I'm ten thumbs in the kitchen."

"Nonsense," said Ellie. "Anyone can learn to cook. You just don't want to, that's all. And there's certainly nothing wrong with that."

Rachel stared at her, as if Ellie had just given her permission to live a long and full life. She hugged her enthusiastically. "That's right, I don't! Oh, thank you, Ellie. Already you're a wonderful friend."

Ellie took some rolls out of a bag and arranged them in a basket while Rachel turned the warming oven on. "You know, I think I wanted to be a cook for only one reason, because my mother never cooked. Ever. And I have spent a lot of my lifetime making sure I never did anything she did, and did everything she didn't, or something like that." She laughed again.

"You and Pete seem to share that goal."

Rachel nodded and poured them each a glass of wine. "That's because we survived childhood only by relying on each other. We made yearly vows we would never raise kids the way our parents did. It wasn't that my folks were bad, not by a long shot. There are many Chicago charities that would go belly-up without my parents' help, for example. They're good people; they simply shouldn't have had children." She took a chocolate mint from the bowl on her marble island and handed it to Ellie, then popped one in her own mouth.

"Do you and Paul have kids?" Ellie asked.

"Not yet." Rachel tapped her tummy, and her whole face opened up into a brilliant smile. "But in seven months we will. I haven't told Pete yet. It's his dessert tonight."

"That's wonderful, Rachel! What a happy surprise."

"And a surprise it surely is. We've been trying like crazy, and I was getting awfully discouraged. And poor, dear Paul was bending over backward, doing everything he could—leaving board meetings the instant I'd call with a 'strike while it's hot' temperature reading, the whole works." She looked momentarily lovestruck, and Ellie smiled at the enormous emotion in her eyes. She wondered if that was what she looked like when she talked about Pete. She knew with absolute certainty that she *felt* that way.

"Anyway," Rachel said, collecting her thoughts, "one of those little wiggly sperm finally found its way home, and soon Paul and I will have our own wonderful, sweet baby. And then, like Pete, we'll be able to pour on all the love and attention we can muster, all those good things our parents thought nannies could do far better than they could."

"I guess we all do a little of that, correcting our parents' mistakes, as we perceive them anyway. My mom is a fantastic mother, I think, but there are always a few things you see that you want to change when you step into that role."

Rachel nodded, sampling the herbed rice. "Yes, I think you're probably right. But there were some definite voids in the Webster household that may surpass the normal mistakes. And those are the ones Pete and I will make sure our kids don't have."

"Like children being raised by hired help."

"I think the bigger thing is not having parents there when you need them, that sort of thing." She laughed to lighten the mood. "I can see Pete has shared his wisdom on this with you. Sometimes he goes a little overboard, but his intentions are good. He loves those kids so much. You can't imagine what he was like when they were each born. And then that . . ." Rachel paused, bit back the words that seemed to be straining to get out, and said calmly, "But then Elaine left. Things have been rough, because Pete's adamant that his kids have as normal a life as possible, and that's tough when there's only one of you doing it."

Ellie sipped her wine and nodded.

"Lucy tells me they've been spending time with you," Rachel said carefully.

"Some."

Rachel grabbed some hot pads and pulled a perfect salmon fillet from the oven. She set it carefully on a hot plate, then checked the restaurant's instructions for her next task. "Well," she said after stirring the dill sauce for the salmon, "they're both great kids. Especially considering the fact that their mom left on a plane one day to go to New York for a job and never came back."

"She did that?"

Rachel nodded. "She did that." She took a small swallow of wine and continued. "Elaine was—is—truly a beautiful woman. Looks a bit like you, in fact, although there's something far more . . . more *welcoming* about your beauty. Anyway, one day she was shopping in Water Tower Place and a man came up, gave her his card, and suggested she call him about modeling. That was that. She contacted the agency, hopped on a plane, and never came back."

Ellie was numb. She knew it hadn't been a pleasant

parting, and she knew Elaine didn't seem to care about mothering much, but this . . . this was abandonment. Her heart ached for Pete's pain.

"Elaine," Rachel went on, "was an ambitious woman. Pete thought she was determined to be a good friend, a good wife, a good mother. His own determination was absolute—he *knew* he'd be a good husband and father. But Elaine discovered that what she and Pete wanted out of life wasn't the same thing after all."

"So she left."

"Yes."

"That's horrible."

Rachel nodded. "It was awful. Especially for P.J. But it happened a lifetime ago. So that's where we should leave it, in that other life. But it does explain some things about my twin brother, whom I love dearly, and I think you have a right to know those things. Now, how about if you flash your magic wand and make that sauce on the stove thicken, and then, thanks to Goldie's Gourmet Take-Out Heaven, we can eat."

On the way home, Ellie thought over her conversation with Rachel. They couldn't have talked as they had, she knew, if there hadn't been that instant liking for each other, that sudden feeling of mutual trust. But she believed Rachel's talking about Pete the way she had had been deliberate, in the same way Fran had been deliberate. Well-intentioned loved ones, that's what these people were, people who cared about their lives and where they were headed.

And then there were she and Pete, the objects of all these good intentions, talking around and above and below their futures as if to do so were to make them disappear.

TWELVE

Once the taping of Ellie's cooking shows began, she and Mary Elliot knew without a doubt that the series was going to be successful. There was a chemistry between the two women that defied defeat.

"Ambitious broads," Mary laughed one day as they wrapped up that day's taping. "That's what some folks would call us."

Ellie shook her head and slumped into a chair. "Such a jaded expression. The fact is, we're good at what we do. We work hard. Therefore we deserve to succeed. And it doesn't have anything to do with gender."

"Except that *our* gender should be having children and driving carpools."

Ellie frowned. Mary's words tugged at so many disquieting thoughts inside her that she had no ready reply. Her thoughts turned inward, to troubling issues that she and Pete hadn't voiced because they were difficult to articulate. And because to articulate them was to deal with them.

She had been over at his house the weekend before so he could try out a new omelette recipe on her. P.J. had been at a friend's, and Lucy at a birthday party, so they had had a wonderful hour in the quiet, lovely home, just the two of them. She smiled at the memory. The day had been autumn at its finest: crisp, cold air with a bright sun to warm your face, and yards covered with blankets of colorful leaves. They had pulled heavy wool sweaters over their jeans and drunk steaming mugs of coffee out on the back terrace. When the coffee was gone, Pete had pulled her onto his lap and wrapped his arms around her, giving her his own special brand of warmth.

Then the phone had rung.

It was one of Pete's partners in the advertising firm, wanting Pete to come in for an hour. Some emergency decisions that couldn't wait, the man said. Ellie told him she'd fill in, pick the kids up at the appointed hour, and bring them home.

Lucy was thrilled when Ellie drove up, and insisted on introducing her to every little friend. Ellie loved the chore, enjoyed seeing the light in Lucy's eyes, hearing her animated chatter, her high, light giggle, and she especially loved the quick kisses that were dropped so freely on her cheek.

A few days ago it had happened again. This time she'd been home, sorting through recipes that she might be able to use in a cookbook. Pete called to say he had an emergency meeting at the office, and though he knew it was an inconvenience, he wondered if there was any way at all she could take Lucy to the dentist. He wouldn't ask, except when Lucy had heard he couldn't take her himself, she had asked for Ellie. She was a little afraid of the dentist; Ellie could handle the fear.

The tug inside her was strong. She needed to work on the cookbook outline and get it to her publisher. And she needed to check in at the studio about some minor details. She grappled with going, but only for a minute, then told Pete yes.

The troubling part about it all was that she loved being with the kids. Her business was a child too, though, growing just as fast, and behaving just as unpredictably. She wasn't sure how many children she could handle.

"Earth to Ellie, come in."

Ellie looked up with a start. Mary was standing across from her, laughing. "You were truly in another world."

Ellie smiled. "Sometimes that happens. I'm back now. Sorry."

"It was hard to tell from the look on your face whether the world you were in was good or bad."

"It was a lovely world," she said, more to herself than to Mary. "But maybe it's not mine to have. I don't know . . ." Her voice trailed off, and when she looked up, Mary was busy with a tape, and several technicians had walked into the room. The talk, blessedly, was about camera angles and sound functions and music tapes. Ellie brightened up and joined in. This she could handle.

❖————————————❖

Ellie had requested that the tapings be finished before Thanksgiving. With hard work and some sacrifice, they were, leaving her with time to cook.

Thanksgiving dinner was always at Ellie's mother's house.

As a child, Ellie had liked Thanksgiving as much as Christmas. She and her brothers and sisters put on an annual play for the grown-ups, rehearsed while the adults were busy gabbing in the kitchen and poking the turkey and drinking her uncle Marty's apple wine. In recent years enough nieces and nephews had sprung up to take over the dramatic honors, while a new bunch of adults joined the old and took over kitchen duties and the apple wine.

This year was no different, and after hours in a steamy kitchen on Thanksgiving morning, Ellie had finally finished the mincemeat, pumpkin, and pecan pies that would be her contribution to the meal.

She slipped off her apron and hung it on its hook, and her thoughts turned automatically to Pete. It was a given that when she had more than ten seconds to spare, she went to Pete, although it was more often a mental connection these days than a physical one.

The day before, in between a dozen other things, she had tried several times to reach him. He'd been in meetings, though, and when he had called her back, she'd been at the television studio. So they had talked through answering machines, leaving generic messages that were unsatisfactory and left Ellie feeling empty and frustrated.

She knew Pete and his children were having Thanksgiving dinner with Rachel and Paul. That was one tradition, he had said, that he and Rachel had in place. Their own childhood Thanksgivings had been spent at the country club. P.J. and Lucy liked it at their aunt and uncle's because Paul and Rachel made it a warm, family kind of day. They built a big fire and roasted marshmallows and chestnuts, and Paul read the kids a story about the Pilgrims. Rachel even did a turkey, Pete had told her. And it didn't taste too bad; it was her one culinary accomplishment.

Impulsively Ellie went to the phone. If she couldn't see him, at least she could hear his voice, wish him a happy Thanksgiving. But the line was busy, and she hung up. She checked over the pies lining the counter. As usual, she'd made enough for a good part of Chicago. Extras. Of course! She'd run a couple out to Pete. She had an hour to spare, a minor miracle in itself, and that would be the perfect way to spend it. They probably already had pies, but at least a part of her would be there. And she knew the past couple of weeks had been as tough on Pete as they had been on her. He wanted things to be simple, their time together predictable, but she couldn't promise him that right now. Although he tried to be patient with her, she knew his patience was wearing thin. A surprise Thanksgiving visit just might do the trick.

In forty minutes she was in his circular driveway, her car filled with warm, fragrant pies that steamed the windows. In the side drive she spotted P.J., dressed in a heavy woolen sweater, shooting baskets at the low hoop Pete had put up for him. She watched him for a minute, then got out of the car and walked around a clump of bushes toward him. "Hi, P.J.," she said. "You're looking good."

He glanced at her, then back to the basket. "We won two games already." He shot the ball up against the metal rim. It spun around, then fell through and bounced back in Ellie's direction.

She caught it, then danced a dribble to the hoop and threw the ball up.

P.J. watched, frowning. When the ball fell through the hoop, he caught it and looked at her again. "I didn't know you were a lefty. Me too."

"My pa always said lefties make the best athletes."

P.J.'s brows went up. "Like who?"

"Well, there's Bill Russell for starters. And Lefty Gomez, Stan Musial, Ted Williams. And those are just off the top of my head."

P.J. 's brows went up farther. He cocked his head. "How do you know that stuff, Ellie?"

"Before my pa died, he and I had season tickets to the Chicago Bulls games. Just the two of us. I like some sports. And my brother Danny plays everything, so he teaches me too."

P.J. smiled, a slightly crooked smile that hit Ellie right in the middle of her heart. "Is your dad home?" she asked around the lump in her throat.

"He's inside." P.J.'s frown came back. "He's trying to fix a dumb turkey."

P.J. turned away and went back to shooting baskets, and Ellie headed for the house. Fixing turkey? Rachel did the turkey, Pete had said. She went around to the kitchen door and knocked lightly, then opened it and peeked through the utility room into the kitchen. "Pete?" she called.

"Ellie!" There was relief and frustration and delight in Pete's voice, and in a second she was wrapped in his arms with her head tight against his chest. She breathed in the pungent odors of onions and thyme and garlic.

Finally she pulled away. "What's going on, Pete?" His shirt was smudged with grease stains, his face tense.

"I'm cooking a damn turkey."

"I thought Rachel—"

"Those plans changed." He wrapped an arm around her shoulders and pulled her into the kitchen. "Come in and sit with me while I try to figure this thing out."

"I brought you some pies, but I'm due at my mother's in a half hour—"

His face seemed to fall at her words, but then he smiled and motioned toward a stool. "Okay, then sit for five minutes. And the pies will be great. Thanks. It may be all we eat."

"What happened with Rachel's?"

"Paul's father had a slight stroke, so they flew to Boston yesterday to be with his parents. The kids and I are having Thanksgiving here."

"Oh, Pete—"

"It's okay. We're doing fine," he said abruptly.

"A Thanksgiving dinner is a lot to bite off, Pete. Why not take them to a restaurant? The kids won't care."

"No." The word shot out like a bullet.

Ellie looked around. The kitchen was a mess. Cookbooks were piled up on the island, and bowls, measuring cups, and food littered the counter. The top-of-the-line Viking stove was covered with grease. She frowned. "Where's the turkey?"

He nodded toward the refrigerator. "It's been thawing. I was just about to take it out."

She opened the refrigerator door and looked in. A huge twenty-pound bird lay on a tray on the center shelf. "When did you put it in here?" she asked.

"Yesterday."

She touched it lightly with her index finger. It was, as she had suspected, frozen solid. She looked over her shoulder at Pete, then at the mess he had made of the kitchen. Shutting the refrigerator door, she walked briskly over to the counter. She noticed P.J. standing at the back door, the basketball in his hands, watching her.

"Where's Lucy?" she asked, her mind jumping ahead, taking charge.

"Upstairs getting dressed," Pete said.

"Okay, here's what we'll do. You change that smelly shirt, Pete; I'll check on Lucy. P.J., you put the ball away, help your dad dump these dirty dishes in the sink, and then we're all going to my mother's house."

Pete stood still, a frown drawing his eyebrows together.

P.J. spoke up first. "No," he said. "I want to stay home."

"He's right, Ellie," Pete said. "We'll stay here. It's planned."

Ellie didn't waver. With her eyes on P.J., she said to Pete, "P.J. will be fine, Pete. Trust me."

"I don't think—" Pete began, but she interrupted.

"Good. Don't think, Webster. I'll do that today. But we need to move it. The kids won't want to miss the play." A swish of Snuf's tail swept across her leg. She looked down. Snuf was pressed against her, his mournful face looking up at her, his eyes huge.

She shook her head and looked over at P.J. He was watching her closely, his eyes full of challenge. She shrugged. "Okay. Snuf can come too. It's Thanksgiving, after all."

They piled into Pete's Explorer—the kids, the dog, the pies, and the adults—and in between giving Pete directions, Ellie led the kids in a rollicking chorus of "Over the River and Through the Woods." Lucy and Ellie sang the loudest, but Pete and P.J.'s voices could be heard trailing by only a few notes.

The Livingston family home was on a long, tree-lined street in one of the city's neatly cared for blue-collar neighborhoods. The house was large and plain with a huge front porch overlooking a yard that was perfect for touch football. The backyard was small with an alley bordering the far side, but it had enough room for Margaret's garden and two old gnarled trees, one holding up an ancient tree house and the other supporting a rope swing.

"It used to be a farmhouse," Ellie explained. "That was before the city grew up around it and divided all this land into little parcels." Her pa, she told the kids, used to tell them that the shed in the backyard was the very place where Mrs. O'Leary's cow kicked over the lantern and started the Great Chicago Fire.

Lucy was enthralled, and even P.J. had trouble hiding the fact that he was impressed.

The house was already full of people, and at first the kids hung back, but Ellie knew it wouldn't last long. In minutes Lucy and P.J. had been claimed by several of her nieces and nephews and shuttled off to meet the others and join in a game of hide-and-seek. Pete looked over at Ellie as the kids ran out of the room. "Ellie . . ."

She heard the emotion in his voice. "I love you too," she said simply. Tucking her arm in his, she pulled him and Snuf into the hot, steamy kitchen, where laughter mingled with aromas that sent Pete's salivary glands into orbit. Snuf curled up beneath the kitchen table, the perfect place to catch fallen food, and thumped his tail as if he had been born there.

Pete was welcomed by everyone with almost as much enthusiasm as the two twenty-two-pound turkeys that Margaret Livingston was cooking in her blackened fifty-year-old oven. Ellie's family accepted his help in lifting birds, uncorking wine bottles, and passing trays of tiny stuffed mushrooms, but no one accepted his thanks for having his family for dinner.

"Each person here adds in some way to our blessings," Margaret told him matter-of-factly.

During a rare moment alone, Pete wandered out onto the front porch. Ellie's youngest brother, Danny, had organized the kids in a quick game of touch football before dinner. Pete spotted P.J. right in the middle of the pack, shouting and cheering and scrambling after the ball. His cheeks were flushed and his eyes bright. He was having the time of his life.

Ellie saw Pete through the window, grabbed a jacket, and joined him. "Hi, there," she said, nuzzling up behind him.

Pete looked over at her, then back out to the kids. "P.J. is in seventh heaven."

"Are you?"

"Pretty close." He wrapped his arm around her. "It was nice of your family to take us in like this."

"Such a way to put it. You and P.J. and Lucy aren't waifs."

"Nor are we Livingstons."

"You're important to me. That's—"

"That's not the same. You know it, too, Ellie." He looked back out at the kids playing. "Ellie, I think it's time you and I did some serious talking. We've both been very good at living for the moment, but—"

"Pete dear, there you are." It was Ellie's mother, beaming at them both as she stepped out onto the porch. "I need those strong arms of Pete's for a minute, Ellie. The other men have deserted me for some television ball game and Tom Turkey won't wait until halftime. Would you mind?"

Ellie watched Pete walk off to her mother's aid, and she wondered if this was fate stepping in again, allowing her some breathing time. But deep down she knew that wasn't fair; this couldn't be left to fate anymore. Pete was right. This was his happiness she was playing with. Her happiness. And now they'd gone and pulled P.J. and Lucy into it as well. And her family too. Everything was connected, woven into this intricate web that had been allowed to expand by happenstance and emotion and . . . and fate.

"Ellie?" It was Lucy, standing in the doorway, her face painted green and large bare twigs attached to her tiny arms with green silk ribbons. "I'm a tree," she said proudly.

"You're a wonderful tree," Ellie said, smiling.

"Time for the play, Aunt Ellie," Sara said, coming up behind Lucy. "Everyone's waiting in the living room. C'mon, Lucy. You're the most important piece of scenery."

Ellie took the little tree's hand and walked with her into the big, drafty living room. Lucy hurried off, eager to stand in her appointed place in front of the fireplace, and Ellie sat in a straight-backed chair off to the side. The children presented their new-age version of the first Thanksgiving, complete with crystal-gazing Pilgrims, Indians with peace symbols painted on their cheeks, tinkling wind chimes hanging from Lucy the tree, and nephew Casey's twelve-string guitar playing loudly in the background.

Pete stood in the back of the room, watching it all, his daughter, his son, and this large family that passed out love and affection as easily as they breathed air. And over to the side was Ellie, beautiful Ellie, her face pensive, touched with a blend of emotion he couldn't read.

What had they done, he wondered, the two of them? What had their loving wrought? Surely something this rich and satisfying had to be good, had to fit into a life that went beyond Big Sur, beyond just the two of them. He looked at Ellie again, and the power of his gaze drew hers across the heads of the others. She half-smiled, then nibbled on her full bottom lip, a now familiar gesture that tugged at his heart. For a moment he felt a longing that was so poignant, so overwhelming, he had to lean against the door frame to steady himself.

The sound of applause broke the moment, and chairs skidded along the hardwood floors. Pete straightened and joined in the clapping.

After the play received a standing ovation, dinner was announced. Fran attached herself to Pete's arm and hustled him into the dining room, and he felt his equilibrium return.

Everyone crowded eagerly around the giant make-shift table. Margaret offered a prayer of thanksgiving for the food, for good health, and most of all for the loved ones all gathered together in her home.

And then the food was passed—endless platters of turkey and dressing; mashed potatoes with the gravy served in a ceramic turkey; sweet potatoes and crisp beans with dill; homemade rolls and acorn squash with cinnamon and melted butter dribbled on top. There was no time for serious thoughts, only serious eating.

Hours later, when dishes were done, more games played, a few tears of tired kids wiped away, Ellie and Pete bundled Lucy, P.J., and Snuffleupagus into the Explorer and took their leave.

The sky was dark over the lake as they headed north to Pete's house. Ellie rested her head against the seat and gave a satisfied sigh.

A tired, contented voice in the backseat broke the silence. "Ellie . . ." P.J. said tentatively.

"What, P.J.?"

"This was, you know, fun today." There was a long pause, then a quiet "Thanks."

"Sure." Ellie smiled and kept her eyes focused on the road ahead. The tear that meandered down her cheek was hidden in the blackness of the night.

THIRTEEN

Pete and Ellie were nearly as bone-weary as the children when they pulled up in Pete's driveway. Thoughts of a serious talk were long forgotten, replaced by more urgent tasks, such as putting tired kids to bed.

Pete carried Lucy upstairs while Ellie helped P.J. lug in the sacks of leftovers that Margaret had sent home with them.

"My basketball tournament starts next week," P.J. said.

Ellie smiled as she piled the foil-wrapped turkey into the refrigerator. "That's great, P.J. I bet you're excited."

He nodded, his hair falling down over his forehead. "I'm point guard," he said with some importance.

"And you're good. Your dad told me."

"There's the schedule." He pointed to a printed sheet attached to the refrigerator with a magnet. "Can you come?"

Ellie looked at the dates. They were circled in red magic marker and highlighted in yellow. Important dates to P.J. "I'd like to. I think I might make a game or two."

He nodded. "Okay." He gave her the lopsided smile that she saw every now and then on Pete's face. It meant he was pleased and a little embarrassed. It was the kind of smile that you could still see when you closed your eyes.

When Ellie finally got to bed that night, she thought of it again, the smile on P.J.'s face, and a small fear ran through her body, chilling her. She pulled the blankets up to her chin, but the chill didn't go away. Neither did the fear, a fear of not doing right by a small, vulnerable boy with a fragile smile.

For the next week Ellie worked nonstop on a detailed draft for her cookbook. Pete was busy with work, the kids, and P.J.'s basketball team, and the only time they seemed to be able to snatch for themselves were odd moments during the day and phone calls late at night.

"I hate this," Pete said one day. They were sitting in her kitchen, Pete in his suit on his way to a meeting, and Ellie in sweats, surrounded by stacks of notes that cluttered the island. Strong coffee scented the air.

"I hate it too," Ellie admitted. "But surely once we get through this busy month, things will get better."

"Do you really think so?"

She shrugged.

"I don't think it will, El."

"I don't know."

"Ellie . . ." He paused, then looked at the cellular phone sitting on the island. "May I?"

She nodded. He punched in his office number, told the receptionist he wouldn't be back for an hour, then hung up and faced Ellie. "Listen, Ellie, I've been doing some serious thinking these last few days."

"You have time to think?" she said in a halfhearted attempt to lighten the mood. Something heavy had moved into her heart, and she couldn't seem to dislodge it.

"Yeah, I have time to think. I think about you constantly, Ellie."

She felt the sting of sudden tears behind her lids. Damn, where had they come from? She nodded. "I know. Me too, Pete. I don't like things they way they've been these last couple of weeks. I miss you terribly."

"Good." He managed a small smile, then it faded. "Ellie," he said slowly, "Ellie, I love you. It's something, I don't know, something I didn't expect. At least not with such enormity about it."

Ellie was nodding as her own emotion bubbled to the surface. "I know," was all she could say.

"And the two of us have been moving through the days trying to keep things the same, pretending our love is still this small, private thing we can hold on to tightly."

"Yes."

Pete didn't touch her, but his eyes bore right down

into her soul. "It's grown, Ellie. It's grown beyond us."

"It was so easy in Big Sur," she said. "You, me, and this incredible, joyful feeling. And then . . . then it seemed to spin out of control."

"Maybe it's not out of control, it's just bigger than we are."

Her eyes locked with his. "Pete, I love you so, so much. I didn't think I'd ever experience the kind of joy you've given me."

He tipped her chin up with two fingers. "It's special, what you and I have, Ellie. One of those things, I think, that only happens once in a lifetime. El, I want to marry you."

Ellie was still. The old clock above her stove ticked loudly in the silence, as magnified as the beating of her heart.

Pete continued. "We're missing out on so much of each other's lives. I want us to be together, Ellie. I want to wake up in the morning and see you next to me in bed. I want to hold you at night before I go to sleep. I want being with you to be the heart of my life and not just stolen moments."

Ellie couldn't breathe easily. The air around her suddenly seemed thin.

"I want us to be a family. You, me, Lucy, and P.J."

"Pete—"

"I know the timing isn't the best, but going on this way doesn't make sense anymore either. It's becoming entangled. We're pulling others into our relationship, just like you do when you're a family. We're building a future without admitting to it, and either we need to *not* do that, El, so people don't end up being hurt, or—"

"I love you so much," she said softly.

Pete touched her hand, only that much, because he knew he couldn't trust himself right now. He was on the edge of a cliff, unsure of the direction he was going. "And I'm pressuring you, dear Ellie, something I swore I wouldn't do. But you're attached to my heart, and I can't float like this anymore, not knowing what our future is, what we're building here, *if* we're building anything—"

"Pete, you and I . . . we barely have time for each other right now. How would I manage a house? Two children?"

"We'd manage, Ellie. We'd simply have to work it out. Make compromises." He forked his fingers through his hair and stared out the window for a minute, then looked back at her. "Saying this, putting it out before us like this, is damn hard. It changes things. It—it's a terrible risk, because I don't know what you'll decide. But I have to do that, for me, for the kids. I have to take the risk." He checked his watch, then sought her eyes again. "Ellie, I have to go. And you need some time alone with all this anyway." He leaned over and kissed her gently, then pulled away and said, "No matter what, I love you, Ellie, more than I ever imagined I could love."

And then he was gone.

It was the long shadows stretching across the dark kitchen that pulled Ellie from the counter stool hours later. She didn't know how long she had been sitting there. A day? A lifetime? A shadow at the back door jarred her, and she stood quickly, her heart beating rapidly. He'd come back, Pete had come back. And everything was going to be fine. They would be again the way they'd been . . .

But it was Fran who knocked lightly, then pushed open the door and walked into the dark kitchen. "Who died?" she asked, flicking on the light switch. Seeing Ellie's face, she rushed to her side. "My Lord, Ellie, what's wrong?"

Ellie slumped back down on the stool. She ran her fingers through her hair. "Franny, you warned me of this, and I wouldn't hear you. I love him so much that I wouldn't hear you, because if I had, I would have had to admit that I can't be what Pete needs. I can't be to Lucy and P.J. what he wants for them. He thinks I can, but I can't."

Fran wrapped her arm around her younger sister and pushed her hair back from her face. "Dear Ellie—"

"Fran, I don't know what to do."

"You'll do what's right for you, and what's right for Pete."

"This feeling I have, this enormous, beautiful feeling—how can it be so complicated, Fran?"

"Love is complicated. It's got all these tentacles that reach out and make all sorts of connections. You can't have it as a pure thing, Ellie. It's a package."

"And Pete's package is so complicated. It's Pete's

expectations. It's those two beautiful children, and their needs, their lives—"

Fran nodded. "And it's yours, too, Ellie. Your needs, your life."

"They need more than I can give, Fran."

"I don't know about the kids, El, but I know Pete. I know he aches for the hurt his kids have already gone through. And I know he'd die before they went through it again."

The tears that had collected for hours finally fell, gentle, sad rivers that ran over Ellie's cheekbones, down her chin, and onto the sheets of paper littering her desk. She sat still, not disturbing the flow.

They met in a lakeside park near Pete's office. Ellie had asked for that. It was neutral, she thought, and a cold wind was blowing in off the lake that brought a stark reality with it.

When she saw Pete striding toward her, though, his collar up against the harsh wind, his big brown eyes seeking hers, she crumbled inside.

He stopped a few feet from her. His face was long, a tired face. There was a furrow between his brows, and she clenched her fists to keep from touching it, smoothing it out.

He forced a smile. "Hello, Ellie."

She tried to answer, but her words were stopped by the enormous lump in her throat. She sucked in a cold, bracing lungful of air and met his eyes.

"Ellie—"

She shook her head, fighting tears. "No, Pete. Let me . . ." The words, they had all been there over the past few days, churning around in her head constantly. Every awful, heartbreaking one of them. But where were they now?

She tried again. "Pete, you were right. I was trying to pull you into my own little fantasy world and lock us both up there, safe and sound." She looked at him with great sadness. "But we couldn't stay there forever, could we?"

Her voice dropped, and when she spoke again, Pete had to strain to hear her.

"Your love is a gift I'll have the rest of my life, Pete. But I can't mess up your life, and I'm afraid that's what I would do."

"Ellie, you *are* my life. An enormous part of it, anyway."

She looked beyond him at the frigid waves of the lake, gray and angry today. How could she do this? How could she give up her one great love? She bit down on her lip, forced herself to look back to Pete, and began again.

"Pete, I know what you've suffered, you and the kids, and I can't risk causing you more pain. You know me, my love for my business, my need to finally succeed. I'm not the sort of woman you want for a wife or a mother. I wouldn't always be there for you and your children, and you'd come to resent that. And then, I don't know, maybe I'd begin to resent things too.

"You want a certain kind of person to mother your kids, and you should have that. I don't think

I can be that person. Not right now. Maybe never. I don't know how . . . I don't know how we could get over the hurdles, not without someone getting hurt in the process. And what if it's the kids? I love them too much already to hurt them, Pete, or to compromise their childhood."

Pete was silent, his eyes never leaving her face. Inside he was cold and hollow.

"As huge as our love is," she went on, "I'm not sure it's big enough to shoulder the kinds of compromises we'd each have to make. I don't know—" her words were tossed about on the breeze, and when they reached her ears, Ellie didn't recognize them. Another person was doing this, a stranger was causing the anguish she was seeing on Pete's face. And then, as she stared at him, the anguish became flecked with anger.

Pete felt the anger coming, and it brought with it a soothing balm. "This is it, then," he said.

That voice, too, Ellie thought, was a stranger's. Not Pete's. Not *her* Pete's. "Pete—" She wanted him to say something, to come up with a solution that would make everything all right. Instead, she saw the warmth in his incredible mahogany eyes turn as cold as the winter ground.

She felt her throat tighten and clog with tears. "Oh, Pete." Her voice was filled with despair.

Pete looked at her and rubbed his cheek, trying to hang on to his anger. It was a life raft, he thought vaguely. Beneath it was the enormous ocean of his love for this woman, a love he had no idea what he would do with. But he needed to do something, so he forced himself to look at Ellie, and he forced himself to say good-bye, and he forced himself to turn and walk slowly over the hard, cold ground into a world that would be forever changed.

When Ellie missed her appointment with Mary Elliot the next day, the producer's assistant called and asked if she was all right.

Ellie nodded, as if her robotlike movements could be seen over the phone. "Yes," she finally managed, although her voice was hoarse and raw.

"You sound ill," the woman said.

"I'll be all right," she said numbly. But she wouldn't. She would never be all right. Three days with little sleep, with no joy, without Pete, had stretched into a hell she could never have imagined. She had cooked for hours: breads and chocolate cakes, stews and soups and casseroles. There was no solace, though, even in that. This time the demons refused to budge.

Fran had come over, and her mother, and even Danny, who told her frankly that she was making the biggest mistake of her life.

She thought about Pete all the time, when she was working at the studio, when she was teaching her course, when she was sitting alone, staring at walls and wondering how so much joy could have evaporated so quickly.

And she thought about P.J. and Lucy. About Rachel. About Snuf. What had Pete told the kids? she wondered. She feared they would think she had abandoned them as their mother had, then consoled herself with the fact that she hadn't been around that much, had only begun to be a part of their lives. And that thought brought yet another river of tears.

Rachel called one morning and asked if she could stop by for a cup of coffee. "Paul's my coffee maker and he's out of town," she said briskly. "The damn stuff I brew tastes like ditch water."

A few hours later she was at Ellie's door. "My Lord," she said when Ellie opened it. "You look as bad as he does, if that's possible."

"How is he?" Ellie asked.

"As okay as you are." Rachel followed Ellie back to the kitchen.

"And the kids?"

Rachel shrugged. "P.J. and Lucy are resilient. They'll be okay, but they're missing out on a lot. That's what rankles me. You two had such a good thing going. I'd always prayed Pete would find someone as wonderful as Paul. My prayers are finally answered and he blows it."

"No, Rachel, it's not like that. It's me, it's both of us. We each have expectations, goals, all sorts of things that simply don't converge."

"And you have this walloping gift of love."

Ellie smiled sadly.

"Pete won't talk to me about this whole thing, but he's dying inside, Ellie. And you are too. Surely there's a message in there somewhere."

"Fate played a cruel joke on us."

"No. I don't believe in that sort of thing. When love this big happens, it is meant to be." She got up and poured herself another cup of coffee.

"I have moments when I tell myself that," Ellie said, brushing away a tear. "But I don't know how. I really don't know how, and I'm not even sure Pete wants to try. But I do love him. I love him so much, Rachel."

"I know you do, Ellie. And I guess that's why I came, besides the fact that Paul says I can never keep my nose out of other people's business. But the way I see it is this: Pete isn't right about everything. His thinking on what the kids need, the kind of attention they need, is understandable, because of where we came from, but also because of what Elaine did. Your success *scares* him, Ellie, but that doesn't mean he's *right*. I mean you're not Elaine, thank God. And there are ways around these things."

Rachel patted her tummy. "This kid is going to be raised by two parents who love him like crazy, and there'll be no nannies making my decisions, but there'll be times when I won't be there. I mean, Lordy, that's life. And I think Pete knows that, too, deep down. He was just so hurt by Elaine, you see, and so afraid for the kids. But I think he can learn a simple thing such as compromise and maybe a more laid-back approach to parenting."

Ellie looked up at Rachel. The tears were going to start again in a minute, full force.

"I have to go, Ellie. But I had to come and say my

piece, for whatever it's worth. You're the best thing that ever happened to my brother, and I love him too much not to butt in."

She hugged Ellie tightly and then was gone, but her words stayed behind, hanging in the still air.

Each morning Ellie got up thinking this day would be better, that some joy and peace and normalcy would creep back into her life.

But each night she went to bed sad and alone, yearning for the brush of Pete's chin against her cheek, the smell of his bathrobe, the taste of his kiss. She tried to remember what her life had been like before him, but she couldn't. There was no life before Pete. And the knowledge that there wouldn't be again was far too ponderous for her to handle.

"You look like hell!" Fran told her one day in mid-December.

"That opinion is shared by many."

"Something has to be done."

Ellie nodded. She pressed her palms against her forehead to block out the ache that resided there.

"You love him." It wasn't a question, but Fran seemed to need confirmation, so Ellie nodded.

"Ellie, what was that quote Cukie LaCrosse used in her article? Something you said about faith and hope. 'If you have faith and hope, all things are possible. . . .' "

Ellie thought of Cukie LaCrosse and that crazy class. And she thought about hope and faith. And she thought about Pete. There was nothing in life that she believed in more than her love for him. And there was nothing she hoped for more than being with him.

Hope . . . The word rattled inside her head the next day as she got off the el and walked the short distance to the television studio. She was making a guest appearance on a call-in show that day, demonstrating some cooking techniques, then answering questions.

The show's moderator was Lily Bennet, a bright and funny local celebrity, and Ellie was grateful for her animated chatter. She and Lily stood together at the cooking island, and while Ellie demonstrated deboning a chicken, they discussed the fine art of teaching men to cook.

The first caller that Lily took asked not about cooking techniques but about Ellie's courses and how he could sign up. The second call was from a man who wanted to share his own recipe for lobster fricassee, and the third was from a woman whose "man friend" had started Ellie's course convinced that all Chinese food came in little white containers and had come out of it a master chef. Ellie suspected she had just been introduced to Tex's Estelle. She managed to smile at the camera and at Estelle, then began slicing mushrooms for the sauce she was making while Lily talked to the next caller.

The studio suddenly went fuzzy. The voice that filtered into her earphone was deep and weary, and oh so familiar. Ellie's heart stopped, the stirring spoon slipped into the pan, and she looked up, half-expecting

Pete to be standing in front of her. But the only thing in front of her was a camera with a stranger behind it.

Beside her, Lily was asking the caller if he had a question.

He did, he said, and Ellie felt the familiar sting of tears behind her lids.

"Go on," said Lily.

"What kind of menu would you suggest if you've driven away the only woman you will ever love because you couldn't see the forest for the trees?"

"Crow?" Lily said. Laughing, she turned to Ellie. "But that's really a question for our guest. Ellie, how would you suggest the man handle this?"

Ellie could barely talk. The tears were threatening, pushing against her lids. She looked around frantically, spotted an onion, and began cutting it. Then she picked it up, let the tears fall, and explained that for starters, you shouldn't fix anything with onions because it would make you cry and the person might mistake the meaning for your tears.

Lily had to interrupt. Unfortunately, they were out of time, she said. After a few parting comments and thank-yous to Ellie, the cameras' lights went off, the spots faded, and Ellie found herself rushing toward the ladies' room and a fresh supply of tissues.

A long meeting with Mary and Janice Jarvis immediately after the broadcast forced Ellie to put Pete's call out of her head. Syndication. They were talking of syndicating the televised *For Men Only*. But the instant joy that should have come, didn't, and Ellie had to force herself to pay attention.

She left the office hours later hearing only one voice: Pete's. Maybe there was a way, she thought, some way for this all to work out. They were two sensible, smart people. And they had something so many people never, ever experienced. A gift. A precious, once-in-a-lifetime gift. Something, surely, that was far too valuable even to consider throwing away.

There *had* to be a way, she told herself as she unlocked her door and walked into her empty house. There had to, because nothing in her life made sense without Pete to share it.

Without taking off her coat, she called his house, her fingers punching out the numbers automatically. She let it ring for a long time, then finally hung up. She wasn't sure what his phone call meant. Maybe he was just as miserable as she was and simply wanted to make contact. Maybe that was all it was.

She turned on a single light in the kitchen and started for the cupboards. Then she stopped halfway across the room. No. She wouldn't cook. She'd plan, that's what she'd do. She'd sit down and look at things clearly, black on white, and then she'd do what she had to do. She'd fought for things that mattered to her all her life. Why had she ever, even for one single instant, thought she should stop now, when the biggest stakes of all were at issue? She shivered as an unexpected warmth swept through her, then she smiled and looked up at the ceiling. "I know, Pop." she whispered. "I know you're proud of me."

FOURTEEN

When Ellie told Fran the next day, Fran thought it was a brilliant idea.

She promised to continue helping Ellie with the admissions for the cooking courses while Ellie devoted her time to training some cooking instructors. Ellie would take Tex up on an offer he'd made weeks ago for the use of an old building he owned in which candy had once been made. It could easily be converted into kitchens, he had said, and he'd like it to be used. She'd get good teachers, set them up, and that would be that. And the syndication, once she thought about it, would be perfect. She could tape bunches of shows at once, when the time was right for her, then send them on their merry way. And cookbooks she could write at home. Dozens if she wanted to!

Yes, it was all falling into place, everything except the whereabouts of Pete. He still didn't answer his phone, and the kids weren't home either. Ellie was desperate. If she didn't see him soon, she felt she would melt away.

And then, as she opened the refrigerator to get some milk, it hit her. P.J.'s basketball tournament. The one he had asked her to go to. She checked her calendar. Yes. One of the games was that night. But where?

Rachel knew, and was only too happy to give directions. A school near Pete's house, his sister said. Ellie couldn't miss it.

Ellie's entire body was shaking as she walked into the school gymnasium. She was assuming so much, taking so much for granted. What if Pete had put things in place his own way? What if . . . No, she couldn't think of that. She knew how *she* felt, and that was worth fighting for, no matter what.

The crowded room echoed with cheering voices as she edged her way into the gym. The air, thick with the smell of perspiring kids, was hot and close.

No one looked her way as she stood beside the bleachers. She was grateful, because she could feel the tears beginning again. She had thought they were gone, that there couldn't possibly be any left, but she was wrong, and again they began to stream down her cheeks.

Finally a large lady, standing alone near the door, looked over at Ellie and noticed the tears. She moved closer and said in a loud but pleasant voice, "It's not worth crying over, miss. The kids have got to learn that losing is okay too."

"Losing?" Ellie said, looking at the woman. No, she was wrong. Losing wasn't an option at all! Pete was her whole life. She would not lose him.

The woman frowned. "Say, you look familiar," she began, pointing toward Ellie as her face wrinkled up in concentration. While the woman was rummaging through her memory for identification, Ellie slipped away, into the crowded stands. She found space behind a man with broad shoulders and a cowboy hat. Peering around him, she felt her heart stop.

There was Pete, directly across from her, on the other side of the court.

He was kneeling beside the bench, his hand touching a small boy's knee, and he was whispering something into the child's ear. All the while his eyes followed a bunch of wiry bodies as they raced up and down the shiny floor, passing the ball and tossing it toward the hoop. Pete nodded and smiled and shouted approval as a little black-haired boy threw and missed. "Great try, Billy!" she heard him call.

Ellie's heart swelled. Then she saw P.J. stumble and fall with the ball. Her hand lifted to her mouth and she half-stood. She wanted to run to him. To pick him up. To hug him to her chest and ask if he was hurt. But P.J. bounced back up, relinquished the ball to the referee, and with a stab at the air with his tight fist, he ran happily back down the floor. In an instant he had stolen the ball back.

Ellie scanned the onlookers behind Pete. There was Lucy, directly behind her dad, clutching the little Indian doll Ellie had given her.

The air in the room became thinner, Ellie's breathing more labored. Oh, Lord, they were her life! The tears began to fall again, blurring her vision. A whistle blew, the boys collected in a huddle, and she couldn't stand it another minute. Excusing herself, she edged her way around the man in the cowboy hat, down to the gym floor. Just as the boys filtered back into their places, she stepped onto the court and caught Pete's eye.

His eyes shot wide open, and his face lifted in the most glorious smile Ellie had ever seen.

Without a thought or backward glance, without hearing the referee's or the people's shouts, she walked across the shiny floor to Pete, who stood waiting, his arms outstretched.

She barely heard the shrill whistle, and only vaguely saw the striped-shirted man who glared at her, then slapped his arms and yelled, "Technical!" She didn't hear the clapping, the excited shouts of the team, nor Lucy's shriek of pure delight. She was oblivious to everything but Pete's eyes, welling with tears, his arms still stretching toward her.

As she neared the bench, all she saw was Pete, and then all she felt was the warmth of his arms swallowing her up in their embrace. She pressed her cheek to his shirt. "Oh, Pete, my darling Pete. I love you so very, very much."

A chorus of little boys groaned, and through her tears, Ellie spotted P.J. in their midst, groaning the loudest, with a delighted smile on his face.

Pete brushed a strand of hair from her face. "Oh, El." His voice broke. "I can't believe you're here."

"To stay, Pete. Forever. If you'll have me."

"Have you? Oh, my sweet, sweet Ellie." He kissed her again, and when the little-boy groans grew louder, he motioned for his assistant to take over. As Ellie scooped Lucy up in her arms, Pete told P.J. to go back out on the floor and beat the pants off the battlin' Blue Jays, then he followed Ellie out into the hall.

"Forever?" he asked, gathering her and Lucy together into a hug.

Ellie pulled a sheet of paper from her pocket and pressed it into his hands. "Some plans for managing time, making some room to breathe in my life—"

"Funny . . . we've been doing the same."

Lucy grinned. "I feed Snuf; P.J. does garbage," she said proudly. "Dad does carpool and cooks."

Pete kissed his daughter on the top of her head, then looked beyond her to Ellie. "I haven't been thinking too clearly, El, and when you were gone, some things hit me right between the eyes. I thought of your mom, and all those kids, and what was important in it all. It's the hugs and the love and the person who will always be there to let you know you're okay, that you're loved. The rest . . . the rest we can work out."

Ellie could barely talk. "And I'll always be there for them in those ways. Always, forever. For all our children."

Lucy squirmed out of Ellie's arms and went back inside to cheer the team on. Pete and Ellie followed slowly behind.

Pete looked at Ellie as they walked, his eyes filled with love and laughter. "Of course, there is one thing . . ."

Ellie brushed aside the last of her tears. "What's that?"

"It's about that technical. If we lose this game . . ."

"Never." She wrapped her arms tightly around him and looked up into the warmest brown eyes she had ever seen. "There's no way on earth we can lose this game, my darling. No way on earth."

THE EDITOR'S CORNER

Next month, LOVESWEPT is proud to present **CONQUERING HEROES,** six men who know what they want and won't stop until they get it. Just when summer is really heating up, our six wonderful romances sizzle with bold seduction and daring promises of passion. You'll meet the heroes of your wildest fantasies who will risk everything in pursuit of the women they desire, and like our heroines, you'll learn that surrender comes easily when love conquers all.

The ever-popular Leanne Banks gives us the story of another member of the Pendleton family in **PLAYING WITH DYNAMITE,** LOVESWEPT #696. Brick Pendleton is stunned when Lisa Ransom makes love to him like a wild woman, then sends him away! He cares for her as he never has another woman, but he just can't give her the promise that she insists is her dearest dream. Lisa tries to forget him, ignore him, but he's gotten under her skin, claiming her with every caress of his mouth and hands. The fierce demolition expert knows everything about tearing things down, but rebuilding Lisa's trust means fighting old demons—and confessing fear. **PLAY-ING WITH DYNAMITE** is another explosive winner from Leanne.

CAPTAIN'S ORDERS, LOVESWEPT #697, is the newest sizzling romance from Susan Connell, with a hero you'll be more than happy to obey. When marina captain Rick Parrish gets home from vacation, the last thing he expects to find is his favorite hang-out turned into a fancy restaurant by Bryn Madison. The willowy redhead redesigning her grandfather's bar infuriates him with her plan to sell the jukebox and get rid of the parrot, but she stirs long-forgotten needs and touches him in dark and lonely places. Fascinated by the arrogant and impossibly handsome man who fights to hide the passion inside him, Bryn aches to unleash it. This determined angel has the power to heal his sorrow and capture his soul, but Rick has to face his ghosts before he can make her his forever. This heart-stopping romance is what you've come to expect from Susan Connell.

It's another powerful story of triumph from Judy Gill in **LOVING VOICES**, LOVESWEPT #698. Ken Ransom considers his life over, cursing the accident that has taken his sight, but when a velvety angel voice on the telephone entices him to listen and talk, he feels like a man again—and aches to know the woman whose warmth has lit a fire in his soul. Ingrid Bjornson makes him laugh, and makes him long to stroke her until she moans with pleasure, but he needs to persuade her to meet him face-to-face. Ingrid fears revealing her own lonely secret to the man whose courage is greater than her own, but he dares her to be reckless, to let him court her, cherish her, and awaken her deepest yearnings. Ken can't believe he's found the woman destined to fill his heart just when he has nothing to offer her, but now they must confront the pain that has drawn them together. Judy Gill will have you laughing and crying with this terrific love story.

Linda Warren invites you to get **DOWN AND DIRTY**, LOVESWEPT #699. When Jack Gibraltar refuses to help archeology professor Catherine Moore find her missing aunt, he doesn't expect her to trespass on his turf, looking for information in the seedy Mexican bar! He admires her persistence, but she is going to ruin a perfectly good con if she keeps asking questions . . . not to mention drive him crazy wondering what she'll taste like when he kisses her. When they are forced to play lovers to elude their pursuers, they pretend it's only a game—until he claims her mouth with sweet, savage need. Now she has to show her sexy outlaw that loving him is the adventure she craves most. **DOWN AND DIRTY** is Linda Warren at her best.

Jan Hudson's conquering hero is **ONE TOUGH TEXAN**, LOVESWEPT #700. Need Chisholm doesn't think his day could possibly get worse, but when a nearly naked woman appears in the doorway of his Ace in the Hole saloon, he cheers right up! On a scale of one to ten, Kate Miller is a twenty, with hair the color of a dark palomino and eyes that hold secrets worth uncovering, but before he can court her, he has to keep her from running away! With his rakish eye patch and desperado mustache, Need looks tough, dangerous, and utterly masculine, but Kate has never met a man who makes her feel safer—or wilder. Unwilling to endanger the man she loves, yet desperate to stop hiding from her shadowy past, she must find a way to trust the hero who'll follow her anywhere. **ONE TOUGH TEXAN** is vintage Jan Hudson.

And last, but never least, is **A BABY FOR DAISY**, LOVESWEPT #701, from Fayrene Preston. When Daisy Huntington suggests they make a baby together, Ben McGuire gazes at her with enough intensity to strip the varnish from the nightclub bar! Regretting her impulsive words almost immediately, Daisy wonders if the man might just be worth the challenge. But when she finds an abandoned baby in her car minutes later, then quickly realizes that several dangerous men are searching for the child, Ben becomes her only hope for escape! Something in his cool gray eyes makes her trust him—and the electricity between them is too delicious to deny. He wants her from the moment he sees her, hungers to touch her everywhere, but he has to convince her that what they have will endure. Fayrene has done it again with a romance you'll never forget.

Happy reading,

With warmest wishes,

Nita Taublib

Nita Taublib

Associate Publisher

P.S. There are exciting things happening here at Loveswept! Stay tuned for our gorgeous new look starting with our August 1994 books—on sale in July. More details to come next month.

P.P.S. Don't miss the exciting women's novels from Bantam that are coming your way in July—**MISTRESS** is the newest hardcover from *New York Times* best-selling author Amanda Quick; **WILDEST DREAMS,** by best-selling author Rosanne Bittner, is the epic, romantic saga of a young beauty and a rugged ex-soldier with the courage to face hardship and deprivation for the sake of their dreams; **DANGEROUS TO LOVE,** by award-winning Elizabeth Thornton, is a spectacular historical romance brimming with passion, humor, and adventure; **AMAZON LILY,** by Theresa Weir, is the classic love story in the best-selling tradition of *Romancing the Stone* that sizzles with passionate romance and adventure as deadly as the uncharted heart of the Amazon. We'll be giving you a sneak peek at these terrific books in next month's LOVESWEPTs. And immediately following this page look for a preview of the exciting romances from Bantam that are *available now!*

Don't miss these extraordinary books by
your favorite Bantam authors

On sale in May:

DARK JOURNEY
by *Sandra Canfield*

SOMETHING BORROWED, SOMETHING BLUE
by *Jillian Karr*

THE MOON RIDER
by *Virginia Lynn*

"A master storyteller of stunning
intensity."
—*Romantic Times*

DARK JOURNEY
by Sandra Canfield

*From the day Anna Ramey moved to Cook's Bay, Maine,
with her dying husband—to the end of the summer when
she discovers the price of forbidden passion in another
man's arms, DARK JOURNEY is nothing less than
electrifying. Affaire de Coeur has already praised it as
"emotionally moving and thoroughly fascinating," and*
Rendezvous *calls it "A masterful work."*

Here is a look at this powerful novel . . .

"Jack and I haven't been lovers for years," Anna
said, unable to believe she was being so frank. She'd
never made this admission to anyone before. She
blamed the numbness, which in part was culpable,
but she also knew that the man sitting beside her
had a way of making her want to share her thoughts
and feelings.

Her statement in no way surprised Sloan. He'd
suspected Jack's impotence was the reason there
had been no houseful of children. He further suspected that the topic of discussion had something
to do with what was troubling Anna, but he let her
find her own way of telling him that.

"As time went on, I adjusted to that fact," Anna
said finally. She thought of her lonely bed and of

more lonely nights than she could count, and added, "One adjusts to what one has to."

Again Sloan said nothing, though he could painfully imagine the price she'd paid.

"I learned to live with celibacy," Anna said. "What I couldn't learn to live with was . . ."

Her voice faltered. The numbness that had claimed her partially receded, allowing a glimpse of her earlier anger to return.

Sloan saw the flash of anger. She was feeling, which was far healthier than not feeling, but again she was paying a dear price.

"What couldn't you live with, Anna?"

The query came so softly, so sweetly, that Anna had no choice but to respond. But, then, it would have taken little persuasion, for she wanted—no, needed!—to tell this man just how much she was hurting.

"All I wanted was an occasional touch, a hug, someone to hold my hand, some contact!" She had willed her voice to sound normal, but the anger had a will of its own. On some level she acknowledged that the anger felt good. "He won't touch me, and he won't let me touch him!"

Though a part of Sloan wanted to deck Jack Ramey for his insensitivity, another part of him understood. How could a man remember what it was like to make love to this woman, then touch her knowing that the touch must be limited because of his incapability?

"I reached for his hand, and he pulled it away." Anna's voice thickened. "Even when I begged him, he wouldn't let me touch him."

Sloan heard the hurt, the desolation of spirit, that lay behind her anger. No matter the circumstances, he couldn't imagine any man not responding to this woman's need. He couldn't imagine any man having the option. He himself had spent the better part of the morning trying to forget the gentle touch of her hand, and here she was pleading with her husband for what he—Sloan—would die to give her.

A part of Anna wanted to show Sloan the note crumpled in her pants pocket, but another part couldn't bring herself to do it. She couldn't believe that Jack was serious about wishing for death. He was depressed. Nothing more.

"What can I do to ease your pain?" Sloan asked, again so softly that his voice, like a log-fed fire, warmed Anna.

Take my hand. The words whispered in Anna's head, in her heart. They seemed as natural as the currents, the tides of the ocean, yet they shouldn't have.

Let me take your hand, Sloan thought, admitting that maybe his pain would be eased by that act. For pain was exactly what he felt at being near her and not being able to touch her. Dear God, when had touching her become so important? Ever since that morning's silken memories, came the reply.

What would he do if I took his hand?
What would she do if I took her hand?

The questions didn't wait for answers. As though each had no say in the matter, as though it had been ordained from the start, Sloan reached for Anna's hand even as she reached for his.

A hundred recognitions scrambled through two minds: warmth, Anna's softness, Sloan's strength, the smallness of Anna's hand, the largeness of Sloan's, the way Anna's fingers entwined with his as though clinging to him for dear life, the way Sloan's fingers tightened about hers as though he'd fight to the death to defend her.

What would it feel like to thread his fingers through her golden hair?

What would it feel like to palm his stubble-shaded cheek?

What would it feel like to trace the delicate curve of her neck?

What would it feel like to graze his lips with her fingertips?

Innocently, guiltily, Sloan's gaze met Anna's. They stared—at each other, at the truth boldly staring back at them.

With her wedding band glinting an ugly accusation, Anna slowly pulled her hand from Sloan's. She said nothing, though her fractured breath spoke volumes.

Sloan's breath was no steadier when he said, "I swear I never meant for this to happen."

Anna stood, Sloan stood, the world spun wildly. Anna took a step backward as though by doing so she could outdistance what she was feeling.

Sloan saw flight in her eyes. "Anna, wait. Let's talk."

But Anna didn't. She took another step, then another, and then, after one last look in Sloan's eyes, she turned and raced from the beach.

"Anna, please . . . Anna . . . *Ann-nna!*"

SOMETHING BORROWED, SOMETHING BLUE
by
Jillian Karr

When the "Comtesse" Monique D'Arcy decides to
feature four special weddings on the pages of her
floundering *Perfect Bride* magazine, the brides find
themselves on a collision course of violent passions
and dangerous desires.

*The T.V. movie rights for this stunning novel have
already been optioned to CBS.*

The intercom buzzed, braying intrusively into
the early morning silence of the office.

Standing by the window, looking down at the sea
of umbrellas bobbing far below, Monique D'Arcy
took another sip of her coffee, ignoring the insistent
drone, her secretary's attempt to draw her into the
formal start of this workday. Not yet, Linda. The
Sinutab hasn't kicked in. What the hell could be so
important at seven-thirty in the morning?

She closed her eyes and pressed the coffee
mug into the hollow between her brows, letting
the warmth seep into her aching sinuses. The
intercom buzzed on, relentless, five staccato blasts

that reverberated through Monique's head like a jackhammer.

"Dammit."

She tossed the fat, just-published June issue of *Perfect Bride* and a stack of next month's galleys aside to unearth the intercom buried somewhere on her marble desk. She pressed the button resignedly. "You win, Linda. What's up?"

"Hurricane warning."

"*What?*" Monique spun back toward the window and scanned the dull pewter skyline marred with rain clouds. Manhattan was getting soaked in a May downpour and her window shimmered with delicate crystal droplets, but no wind buffeted the panes. "Linda, what are you talking . . ."

"Shanna Ives," Linda hissed. "She's on her way up. Thought you'd like to know."

Adrenaline pumped into her brain, surging past the sinus headache as Monique dove into her fight or flee mode. She started pacing, her Maud Frizon heels digging into the plush vanilla carpet. Shanna was the last person in the world she wanted to tangle with this morning. She was still trying to come to grips with the June issue, with all that had happened. As she set the mug down amid the organized clutter of her desk, she realized her hands were shaking. Get a grip. Don't let that bitch get the better of you. *Oh, God, this is the last thing I need today*.

Her glance fell on the radiant faces of the three brides smiling out at her from the open pages of the magazine, faces that had haunted her since she'd found the first copies of the June issue in a box beside her desk a scant half hour earlier.

Grief tore at her. Oh, God, only three of us. There were supposed to have been four. There *should* have been four. Her heart cried out for the one who was missing.

This had all been her idea. Four stunning brides, the weddings of the year, showcased in dazzling style. Save the magazine, save my ass, make Richard happy. All of us famed celebrities—except for one.

Teri. She smiled, thinking of the first time she'd met the pretty little manicurist who'd been so peculiarly reluctant at first to be thrust into the limelight. Most women dreamed of the Cinderella chance she'd been offered, yet Teri had recoiled from it. *But I made it impossible for her to refuse. I never guessed where it would lead, or what it would do to her life.*

And Ana, Hollywood's darling, with that riot of red curls framing a delicate face, exuding sexy abandon. Monique had found Ana perhaps the most vulnerable and private of them all. *Poor, beautiful Ana, with her sad, ugly secrets—I never dreamed anyone could have as much to hide as I do.*

And then there was Eve—lovely, tigerish Eve, Monique's closest friend in the world, the once-lanky, unsure teenage beauty she had discovered and catapulted to international supermodel fame. *All I asked was one little favor . . .*

And me, Monique reflected with a bittersweet smile, staring at her own glamorous image alongside the other two brides. Unconsciously, she twisted the two-and-a-half-carat diamond on her finger. Monique D'Arcy, the Comtesse de Chevalier. *If only they knew the truth.*

Shanna Ives would be bursting through her door any minute, breathing fire. But Monique couldn't stop thinking about the three women whose lives had become so bound up with her own during the past months. Teri, Ana, Eve—all on the brink of living happily ever after with the men they loved . . .

For one of them the dream had turned into a nightmare. *You never know what life will spring on you,* Monique thought, sinking into her chair as the rain pelted more fiercely against the window. *You just never know. Not one of us could have guessed what would happen.*

She hadn't, that long-ago dawn when she'd first conceived the plan for salvaging the magazine, her job, and her future with Richard. Her brilliant plan. She'd had no idea of what she was getting all of them into. . . .

THE MOON RIDER

by VIRGINIA LYNN

bestselling author of
IN A ROGUE'S ARMS

"Lynn's novels shine with lively adventures,
a special brand of humor
and sizzling romance."
—*Romantic Times*

*When a notorious highwayman accosted Rhianna and
her father on a lonely country road, the evening ended
in tragedy. Now, desperate for the funds to care for her
bedridden father, Rhianna has hit upon an ingenious
scheme: she too will take up a sword—and let the heart-
less highwayman take the blame for her robberies. But
in the blackness of the night the Moon Rider waits, and
soon this reckless beauty will find herself at his mercy,
in his arms, and in the thrall of his raging passion.*

"Stand and deliver," she heard the highwayman
say as the coach door was jerked open. Rhianna
gasped at the stark white apparition.

Keswick had not exaggerated. The highwayman
was swathed in white from head to foot, and she
thought at once of the childhood tales of ghosts
that had made her shiver with delicious dread.

There was nothing delicious about this apparition.

A silk mask of snow-white was over his face, dark eyes seeming to burn like banked fires beneath the material. Only his mouth was partially visible, and he was repeating the order to stand and deliver. He stepped closer to the coach, his voice rough and impatient.

Llewellyn leaned forward into the light, and the masked highwayman checked his forward movement.

"We have no valuables," her father said boldly. Lantern light glittered along the slender length of the cane sword he held in one hand. "I demand that you go your own way and leave us in peace."

"Don't be a fool," the Moon Rider said harshly. "Put away your weapon, sir."

"I have never yielded to a coward, and only cowards hide behind a mask, you bloody knave." He gave a thrust of his sword. There was a loud clang of metal and the whisk of steel on steel before Llewellyn's sword went flying through the air.

For a moment, Rhianna thought the highwayman intended to run her father through with his drawn sword. Then he lowered it slightly. She studied him, trying to fix his image in her mind so that she could describe him to the sheriff.

A pistol was tucked into the belt he wore around a long coat of white wool. The night wind tugged at a cape billowing behind him. Boots of white leather fit him to the knee, and his snug breeches were streaked with mud. He should have been a laughable figure, but he exuded such fierce menace that Rhianna could find no jest in what she'd earlier thought an amusing hoax.

"Give me one reason why I should not kill you on the spot," the Moon Rider said softly.

Rhianna shivered. "Please sir—" Her voice quivered and she paused to steady it. "Please—my father means no harm. Let us pass."

"One must pay the toll to pass this road tonight, my lovely lady." He stepped closer, and Rhianna was reminded of the restless prowl of a panther she'd once seen. "What have you to pay me?"

Despite her father's angry growl, Rhianna quickly unfastened her pearl necklace and held it out. "This. Take it and go. It's all of worth that I have, little though it is."

The Moon Rider laughed softly. "Ah, you underestimate yourself, my lady fair." He reached out and took the necklace from her gloved hand, then grasped her fingers. When her father moved suddenly, he was checked by the pistol cocked and aimed at him.

"Do not be hasty, my friend," the highwayman mocked. "A blast of ball and powder is much messier than the clean slice of a sword. Rest easy. I do not intend to debauch your daughter." He pulled her slightly closer. "Though she is a very tempting morsel, I must admit."

"You swine," Llewellyn choked out. Rhianna was alarmed at his high color. She tugged her hand free of the Moon Rider's grasp.

"You have what you wanted, now go and leave us in peace," she said firmly. For a moment, she thought he would grab her again, but he stepped back.

"My thanks for the necklace."

"Take it to hell with you," Llewellyn snarled. Rhianna put a restraining hand on his arm. The Moon Rider only laughed, however, and reached out for his horse.

Rhianna's eyes widened. She hadn't noticed the horse, but now she saw that it was a magnificent Arabian. Sleek and muscled, the pure white beast was as superb an animal as she'd ever seen and she couldn't help a soft exclamation of admiration.

"Oh! He's beautiful. . . ."

The Moon Rider swung into his saddle and glanced back at her. "I salute your perception, my fair lady."

Rhianna watched, her fear fading as the highwayman swung his horse around and pounded off into the shadows. He was a vivid contrast to the darker shapes of trees and bushes, easily seen until he crested the hill. Then, to her amazement, with the full moon silvering the ground and making it almost shimmer with light, he seemed to vanish. She blinked. It couldn't be. He was a man, not a ghost.

One of the footmen gave a whimper of pure fear. She ignored it as she stared at the crest of the hill, waiting for she didn't know what.

Then she saw him, a faint outline barely visible. He'd paused and was looking back at the coach. Several heartbeats thudded past, then he was gone again, and she couldn't recall later if he'd actually ridden away or somehow just faded into nothing.

And don't miss these fabulous romances from Bantam Books, on sale in June:

MISTRESS
Available in hardcover
by *The New York Times* bestselling author
Amanda Quick
"Amanda Quick is one of the most versatile and talented authors of the last decade."
—*Romantic Times*

WILDEST DREAMS
by the nationally bestselling author
Rosanne Bittner
"This author writes a great adventurous love story that you'll put on your 'keeper' shelf."
—*Heartland Critiques*

DANGEROUS TO LOVE
by the highly acclaimed
Elizabeth Thornton
"A major, major talent . . . a superstar."
—*Romantic Times*

AMAZON LILY
by the incomparable
Theresa Weir
"Theresa Weir's writing is poignant, passionate and powerful."
—*New York Times*
bestselling author Jayne Ann Krentz

OFFICIAL RULES

To enter the sweepstakes below carefully follow all instructions found elsewhere in this offer.

The **Winners Classic** will award prizes with the following approximate maximum values: 1 Grand Prize: $26,500 (or $25,000 cash alternate); 1 First Prize: $3,000; 5 Second Prizes: $400 each; 35 Third Prizes: $100 each; 1,000 Fourth Prizes: $7.50 each. Total maximum retail value of Winners Classic Sweepstakes is $42,500. Some presentations of this sweepstakes may contain individual entry numbers corresponding to one or more of the aforementioned prize levels. To determine the Winners, individual entry numbers will first be compared with the winning numbers preselected by computer. For winning numbers not returned, prizes will be awarded in random drawings from among all eligible entries received. Prize choices may be offered at various levels. If a winner chooses an automobile prize, all license and registration fees, taxes, destination charges and, other expenses not offered herein are the responsibility of the winner. If a winner chooses a trip, travel must be complete within one year from the time the prize is awarded. Minors must be accompanied by an adult. Travel companion(s) must also sign release of liability. Trips are subject to space and departure availability. Certain black-out dates may apply.

The following applies to the sweepstakes named above:

No purchase necessary. You can also enter the sweepstakes by sending your name and address to: P.O. Box 508, Gibbstown, N.J. 08027. Mail each entry separately. Sweepstakes begins 6/1/93. Entries must be received by 12/30/94. Not responsible for lost, late, damaged, misdirected, illegible or postage due mail. Mechanically reproduced entries are not eligible. All entries become property of the sponsor and will not be returned.

Prize Selection/Validations: Selection of winners will be conducted no later than 5:00 PM on January 28, 1995, by an independent judging organization whose decisions are final. Random drawings will be held at 1211 Avenue of the Americas, New York, N.Y. 10036. Entrants need not be present to win. Odds of winning are determined by total number of entries received. Circulation of this sweepstakes is estimated not to exceed 200 million. All prizes are guaranteed to be awarded and delivered to winners. Winners will be notified by mail and may be required to complete an affidavit of eligibility and release of liability which must be returned within 14 days of date on notification and alternate winners will be selected in a random drawing. Any prize notification letter or any prize returned to a participating sponsor, Bantam Doubleday Dell Publishing Group, Inc., its participating divisions or subsidiaries, or the independent judging organization as undeliverable will be awarded to an alternate winner. Prizes are not transferable. No substitution for prizes except as offered or as may be necessary due to unavailability, in which case a prize of equal or greater value will be awarded. Prizes will be awarded approximately 90 days after the drawing. All taxes are the sole responsibility of the winners. Entry constitutes permission (except where prohibited by law) to use winners' names, hometowns, and likenesses for publicity purposes without further or other compensation. Prizes won by minors will be awarded in the name of parent or legal guardian.

Participation: Sweepstakes open to residents of the United States and Canada, except for the province of Quebec. Sweepstakes sponsored by Bantam Doubleday Dell Publishing Group, Inc., (BDD), 1540 Broadway, New York, NY 10036. Versions of this sweepstakes with different graphics and prize choices will be offered in conjunction with various solicitations or promotions by different subsidiaries and divisions of BDD. Where applicable, winners will have their choice of any prize offered at level won. Employees of BDD, its divisions, subsidiaries, advertising agencies, independent judging organization, and their immediate family members are not eligible.

Canadian residents, in order to win, must first correctly answer a time limited arithmetical skill testing question. Void in Puerto Rico, Quebec and wherever prohibited or restricted by law. Subject to all federal, state, local and provincial laws and regulations. For a list of major prize winners (available after 1/29/95): send a self-addressed, stamped envelope entirely separate from your entry to: Sweepstakes Winners, P.O. Box 517, Gibbstown, NJ 08027. Requests must be received by 12/30/94. DO NOT SEND ANY OTHER CORRESPONDENCE TO THIS P.O. BOX.